Witch Madness

"Mistress Bishop," said Magistrate Corwin, "you are accused of being a witch. How say you to this charge?"

"I do not know what a witch is."

Immediately the girls in the circle, who were sitting up front in the room, went into fits. They threw themselves on the floor and shrieked and wailed. They twitched their bodies and howled like forest creatures at the time of the full moon. The howling was a terrible thing to hear. It cut through one's bones with its primitive sound.

Magistrate Hathorne banged the table with his gavel. One of the girls screamed, "I see Bridget's shape up on that beam. Can't you see it? She sits there mocking me!"

At once, the girl's brother sprang out of the crowd of spectators, tore his sword from his side, and attacked the place where his sister pointed.

"He has ripped her cloak!" she cried out. "See? I heard it ripping!"

"I am innocent to a witch!" Bridget Bishop cried. "I know not what a witch is!"

"Take her away," boomed Magistrate Hathorne. And so she was taken.

A Break
With Charity

A Break With Charity

A STORY ABOUT THE

Salem Witch Trials

ANN RINALDI

SCHOLASTIC INC.

New York Toronto London Auckland Sydney
Mexico City New Delhi Hong Kong Buenos Aires

ISBN 0-439-81071-X

12 11   13 14/0

Printed in the U.S.A.   23

First Scholastic printing, October 2005

Designed by Lisa Peters

For my husband, Ron,

who was with me through it all

Acknowledgments

I am indebted to the scholars who researched and wrote the many books I used for reference; to the people at the Essex Institute in Salem, Massachusetts; to the people at the Salem Maritime National Historic Site; to my editor, Karen Grove of Harcourt Brace & Company, for giving me a contract for this book without a word on paper during a time of my life when such faith in me mattered so much; and to my son, Ron, for the use of his library on American and military history, as well as for leading me to my interest in American history in the first place. Gratitude also goes to my agent, Joanna Cole, for her encouragement; to my family for their forbearance; and most especially to my husband, Ron, who accompanied me on research trips and listened to my problems.

Ann Rinaldi
January 7, 1992

Contents

A Break
With Charity

Prologue
1706

I have come early this afternoon to sit, before anyone else arrives, in the quiet of Salem Meetinghouse. It is cool in here, though the August sun beats down outside—even at the end of the day—on corn that stands high in the fields and on fruit trees already laden with their fall harvest.

I am a stranger in this church. Indeed, I have not been here since spring of 1692, so long ago now that it seems but a dim memory, and the girl I was at that time seems certainly like another person. Me and yet not me, that young girl. For she was as innocent to the dangers around her as my own baby daughter who now sleeps peacefully in my arms.

Another world it was back then, although most of us hereabouts live with some mark of the events of that time still upon us. And those marks might as well be a limping leg or a scarred face or lost fingers on one hand, for the way in which so many have been crippled.

As for me, I speak seldom, if ever, of those terrible months of 1692. Nor does my husband. Indeed, I thought I had put them behind me until I came into

1

this church today. When I did, once I entered these portals, it all came rushing back.

Mostly I thought of Mama. And when I first sat down here, with my three-year-old boy beside me and the baby in my arms, it was Mama's face I saw, Mama's voice I heard, like it was yesterday.

Sometimes I miss her so much! I missed her so when I was married. And there are times when I ache for her as I look on my children's faces. But today, when I came into this place, it was more than aching for her or missing her. It was as if her presence was here with me, all around me. And I cried.

This was Mama's meetinghouse, the place she loved so until that fateful day when she stood by Sarah Cloyce as the others shunned Sarah and called Mama a friend of witches. She never came back here after that day. As I look around me now I wonder, should I have come today? Or do I dishonor her memory by doing so?

Oh, I did not want to come! 'Twas my husband bade me do so. "Consider how torn asunder the community still is, even after all these years," he said. "You should go and stand by your neighbors. If only for the sake of our two little ones who will grow up here."

So I said, "Yes, I will go," though in my heart I will never understand why we women are always assigned the task of peacemaking. "I will go, but I will not forgive Ann Putnam. You cannot ask me to do that, husband," I told him. And I wonder, now that I am here, how I can look on her face again without seeing the faces of all whom she destroyed.

The meetinghouse is peaceful, though. And I can see it has not changed from those days of my childhood. It was the Reverend Parris's church back then. But he is long since gone. Since January of 1693, when the townsfolk met to make void his salary.

Reverend Joseph Green took his place when he left. Green was only twenty-two when he came. And though I do not come to hear him preach, I myself have seen him take off his doublet to help a neighbor build a new barn or take up his musket to go out and help hunt wolves on the edge of town. They say he has worked long and hard to heal the community from the effects of what people call "the recent tragedy."

That is the way they refer to the witch madness of 1692. And all the hangings. As if they cannot bear to mention the word *witchcraft* ever again.

They said the word plain enough back then. And said it and said it and said it. Until the hearing was beyond bearing. And until nineteen innocent people were hanged and one was pressed to death and scores lay in prison. Oh, they had no trouble saying the words *Devil* and *witchcraft* back in 1692, did they?

But I must rein in my bitter thoughts. For I was invited here today by Reverend Green.

3

For this day, he said, young Ann Putnam is going to stand in front of the congregation and beg forgiveness for her part in the witch madness.

Beg forgiveness, indeed! After fourteen years! I see no purpose to it. The dead are dead; those who remain behind cannot forget. But then, just as I am about to close my heart against Ann, I recollect my part in the madness that came to our village in 1692. And I know I am as guilty as Ann or any of the girls in that circle of accusers.

Though my name appears not in any of the briefs or letters or public statements written about the witch madness, I was as much a part of the shame of it as any of them.

I stand as guilty as they. For I knew better and did not step forth to try to stop the madness. Certainly not in any manner that counted. I held back, afraid.

Oh, I know learned men also held back until they knew the time was right and there would be no reprisals. It helps me sometimes, knowing that. It helps in my head. But in my heart, where such matters weigh the heaviest, I know how wrong I was.

And that is the real reason I am here today. For if Ann Putnam can come and publicly beg forgiveness—an act I could never do—then surely I can come and bear witness.

The congregation that has assembled all around me while I sit here will forgive her, I know. All of them will forgive her. Even the kinsmen of Rebecca Nurse and the family of Martha and Giles Cory. And all of John and Elizabeth Proctor's children. All those who were most wronged will forgive her and welcome her back into the congregation.

But who will forgive me?

Oh, if I had only known that day so long ago when I stood outside the parsonage in the cold, aching to belong to that circle of girls who did not want me. If I had only known what they were about, truly I would have turned and run the other way!

I would have turned and run across the snow, back to my horse and cart, and dashed away!

I close my eyes now and tremble with the memory. Wishing I could bring it back. Wishing. For I remember just how it was, and where I was standing and what I was feeling in that moment it was given to me to decide what to do.

Given the chance again, I know I would do the right thing. I would run. I know I would!

Wouldn't I?

1

THE WOMAN WHO
WASN'T THERE

✺ THE DAY I MET
Sarah Bibber behind the cluster of trees outside the
parsonage was not a good day. Enough to say there is
never a good time to meet Sarah Bibber. The woman
doesn't open her mouth but toads jump off her tongue,
as my mother would say. Scandalmongering was always Sarah's best talent. I suppose if she were married, the edge would be taken off her tongue. But she
was twoscore and then some, with no prospects, so
she went about Salem Village undoing all the good
she saw. And concocting evil where there was none.

The parsonage was where the Reverend Parris
lived. I was so busy watching the girls gathering

outside his front door that I did not hear Sarah's footsteps behind me.

I peered through the naked trees and bushes, toward the house. The girls had gone inside now, and, as always, I was standing alone in the bone-numbing dusk. Candles were lighted and shining in the windows. The girls would all be warm and safe, sitting around the fire, I thought. Listening to Tituba's stories. And I was out here, alone and friendless, in the bleakness of the early December landscape. And colder for the knowledge that they did not want me than I was from the bite of the wind.

The girls of Salem Village had formed their circle as the cold set in at the end of November in 1691. In the beginning, the circle consisted only of Mary Walcott, Elizabeth Booth, and Susannah Sheldon. And every time I chanced by the parsonage and saw them being admitted by little Betty Parris, who was only nine, and her cousin Abigail Williams, who was eleven, I would wonder why Mary and Elizabeth and Susannah would bother to be friends with the younger girls. For Mary was seventeen, and Susannah and Elizabeth were both eighteen, and they wouldn't even bother to speak to me since I was only fourteen and not worthy of their favor.

Something was going on, I was sure of it. And as I stood there, yearning to be part of it all, I realized that whatever was happening inside was happening only when the reverend and his wife were out, which was often.

For the village was in a sorry state, what with a recent outbreak of smallpox, Indian raids on the fringes of the town, and the devout predicting that Doomsday was upon us. Surely enough to keep any reverend and his wife busy. Mrs. Parris was as occupied with her charitable missions as her husband was, she being the kind of woman who believes that even if Doomsday were upon us, God would expect to find her in her best cap and apron, ministering to the poor until the final moment.

Last week, Mercy Lewis had come and been admitted to the parsonage with the others. And she a maidservant for Thomas and Ann Putnam! The girls had welcomed her into their midst as if she were Queen Mary herself. I stood there behind the trees, shivering with anger that they should accept Mercy Lewis and not me. She was such a sly wench.

And now Ann Putnam was joining the group. Her high-pitched giggle reached me across the snowy field, making my heart numb. Mercy had brought her along, of course. Ann was twelve and sickly. Now there would be trouble. The Putnams were always trouble, except for Ann's uncle Joseph and his wife, Elizabeth. Everybody liked young Joseph and Elizabeth Putnam, mostly because everybody knew Joseph had little to do with his older brother Thomas and Thomas's wife, Ann.

"Her mother's sent her, I'll wager."

I turned to see Sarah Bibber smiling down at me. Snaggle-toothed, the hair under her cap almost all gray, she smelled musty and stale, even in the cold, crisp air.

The woman probably never washes, I told myself. But that was unkindly. And if God was turning His countenance from Salem Village, as Reverend Parris often said at Meeting, it was as likely because of my uncharitable heart as because of anyone else's. But I couldn't help it.

I was not a proper Puritan, I knew that. The heart that beat in my breast was more like my father's than my mother's. But he was a man, a town elder, and a rich merchant. So he could be forgiven his enlightened views while I, a mere girl, could not. I knew that, too.

But it didn't help when my mind took flight in Meeting and I dreamed of being on the *William and Susanna*, my father's brigantine, with my older brother, William, who was twenty-five and world-traveled. And who had little patience with prophecies of Doomsday. So, most of the time, I had feelings no proper Puritan girl should harbor. And lack of charity was one of them.

"You should have announced your presence,

Goody Bibber," I said. "How long have you been standing there?"

"Long enough to hear your thoughts, child."

"No one can hear another's thoughts."

"Are ye sure of that?"

"No, I'm not sure of much these days."

"And why is that, child?"

"Most everyone knows, Goody Bibber, that it's been two months since we've received word from my brother, William. And that each day the *William and Susanna* isn't sighted plotting its course in the distance off Salem Town harbor, hope dims for his return."

"Have faith, child."

"My heart is swept clean of faith. The last we heard of William was when he put ashore at Barbados. That letter told of three Spanish privateers waiting for him on the leeward islands."

"Your brother has captained your father's vessels, I hear, for years now to England, France, Holland, Italy, Newfoundland, and the West Indies. He is a man of courage. He knows what winds will guide him."

"He'll need a higher power than the winds," I said sadly. "The seas are plagued with pirates."

"Is that why ye be standing here, outside the parsonage, so often, then? I've seen ye many a cold afternoon."

I looked up into the lined face to see an unexpected

twinkle in her eyes. "What would brother William have to do with me standing here outside the parsonage?" I asked.

She laughed, a dry, cackling sound. "Well, what do ye think those girls do in there every day, child?"

I looked toward the gray and forbidding outline of the building. "Stories." I sighed. "I heard that Reverend Parris's slave Tituba tells them stories."

" 'Tis far more than stories that cures the useless hours of dullness for those girls," she said knowingly.

"What is it, then? What do they do in there?"

"Fortune-telling," she said. "Tituba is familiar with the black arts. Did not the good reverend bring her back from the West Indies?"

"So they say."

"Fortune-telling," she said again. "Little sorceries. Palmistry. I hear she conjures with sieve and scissors, poppets made of cloth, and candles."

I gasped. "Such practices are forbidden!"

"I hear she reads the leaves of tea."

"In the reverend's own house?"

"Aye."

"And you thought I wanted . . ." I could not even finish the sentence.

"I thought ye were seeking out Tituba to tell ye when brother William will be coming home."

The idea hung in front of me like a bright candle, lighting up the bleak winter afternoon. "Such things are forbidden," I said again, but my voice was weak this time.

She smiled down at me. And between her smile and the beating of my own heart, desire was born. And the night was separated from day. "God reveals all things to us in His own good time," I recited, knowing it was what Mama would say.

"God is ofttimes busy elsewhere. And we must satisfy our own yearnings by whatever means we can until He turns His face to us again."

" 'Tis the Devil's business," I said sharply.

She shrugged. "If my own brother were missing at sea, I'd do all I could to ease the pain in my heart."

"They wouldn't have me inside," I argued.

"Have ye asked?"

"They don't like me."

"Might I ask why?"

Without realizing that I was doing so, I continued to confide in her. "Because my father is a merchant with twenty-one vessels to his name. And because I live in a fine three-story house in Salem Town and not here in the village. And because we eat from pewter and have many servants. But I don't care. There isn't a decent one of those girls in the lot."

She nodded, agreeing. "Then why are ye about here so much? It's three miles from Salem Town to this place."

"I deliver goods from my parents' shop. But not

for the king's shilling. Mama sends needed items to the poor of the village."

"She allows ye to go about with that horse and cart and deliver them alone?"

"No. I usually have our maidservant Ellinor with me. But she was down with quinsy throat this morning, so I came alone."

"And ye just happen to stop at this spot all the time to rest your horse," she said.

"If you must know, yes, that's why I stop here, Goody Bibber," I said.

She sighed. " 'Tis a shame, the way we lie to ourselves and come to believe it," she murmured.

"I'm not lying to myself, Goody Bibber."

"Odd, then, that when I came up behind ye before, I did hear ye thoughts. Enough to know ye is heartsore because they won't let ye join them."

I stared up at her, an angry retort on my lips. Then I saw the slow and benign smile spread across her face, making it almost beautiful in spite of the wrinkles.

"Mayhap ye don't care about the girls. But ye care about Tituba now that I've told ye what she's about, I can see that. Why don't ye ask John Indian to let ye in the back door?"

I looked to where she was pointing. Across the expanse of snow-covered ground that separated us from the parsonage, I could see John Indian, Tituba's husband, chopping wood outside the back door. The steady blows of his ax carried on the cold air and then grew distant as I pondered.

Why, yes, of course! The girls usually took their leave after about an hour. I didn't need them to gain entrance. I was, after all, Susanna English, and our family had never needed anyone's help to gain entrance anywhere.

The thought of my family, my parents, filled me with foreboding. Surely, asking Tituba to read her tea leaves and conjur with sieve and candles to tell me the future would be trafficking with the Devil. What if my parents found out?

Mama would be heartsick. As for my own dear honored Father English (as William and my older sister, Mary, and I called him), well, I knew he was far too enlightened to believe that the Devil was roaming the hills and dales of Salem, as so many others believed these days.

Storms at sea, English pirates seizing his vessels, a cargo of molasses gone bad, Indians attacking his ketches bringing fish back from Newfoundland: these things my father considered natural plagues that beset one in his trade, not visitations from the Devil.

My father's ideas often put him at odds with the town magistrates, selectmen, and ministers. Mama said he was better understood by the merchants of Boston, where he had many friends. Boston was a place of ideas. But ideas were never encouraged in Salem.

For this reason, and because he was loyal to the Church of England, my father would not go to Salem Village Meeting on the Sabbath. He rowed across the bay to St. Michael's Episcopal in Marblehead when weather permitted. And when it did not permit, he prayed alone in the privacy of his home, where he often went about saying there was no religious freedom under the Puritans.

My father always set great store by freedom. But he was always well respected in Salem, nevertheless, and considered a good neighbor, a man to call upon in times of trouble, a man with a clear head, a man of firm purpose.

And of course, folks in Salem always remembered the time he stood with his fellow countrymen in Boston in 1689, when the people sent Sir Edmund Andros, who was then governor, to be imprisoned in the dungeon at Castle William in the harbor.

In Massachusetts Bay Colony, the people had for years been coining their own money and ignoring the navigation acts passed by Parliament and, in general, showing too many signs of being independent. So, in 1684, the Crown took away our charter to punish us.

That charter was second only to the Bible to us because it guaranteed us our land titles. Then the Crown gave us Andros as governor.

He passed harsh taxes and said our land titles were no longer valid now that the charter was gone. So the people imprisoned him in 1689. And my father was one of the men to help draw up our Declaration of the Gentlemen, Merchants, and Inhabitants of Boston and the Country Adjacent, and he stood with the people when it was read aloud.

People marked well that my father did that. Just as they marked well that he put up the money for the journey, on the frigate *Nonesuch*, of the Reverend Increase Mather of Boston. So he could go to England and get us a new charter.

Of course, my father predicted that matters would get worse before they got better between us and the Crown. And we would pay dearly someday for this freedom we so cherish. But he blamed our troubles on neither God nor the Devil.

The sound of a horse's whinny brought me to my senses. Yes, I decided, my father was a man of advanced ideas, but I knew that even he would not approve of trafficking with the Devil.

So, then, I would just have to be sure that neither he nor Mama found out, wouldn't I? For I had, by that time, determined to get in to see Tituba. And if she could give me some good word about William, I would go away satisfied. I would take that good word and keep it as medicine. I would hold it close to me in the middle of the night and tell no one else of it.

"Goody Bibber." I turned to tell her of my decision, but she was nowhere in sight. Gone. I peered through a curtain of snow that I hadn't even realized was falling. How long had I been standing there musing? It was getting on to dark.

There were no footprints. And for a moment I pondered whether she had truly been there or I had dreamed it. Before I could consider the question further, however, I was covering the ground between myself and my horse and cart, to fetch a twist of tobacco for John Indian.

And that is how it started with me. That began my part in the madness that came to our village in the year 1692. But I had no idea of what would transpire once I got in the back door of the parsonage. All I knew was that Tituba told fortunes. And that I wanted to know if William would be coming back to us. Or was he lost, forever, at sea.

William, my beloved older brother, who was always laughing, always bringing joy into the house and lovely trinkets back from his travels for my sister, Mary, and me. Coral shells, books, even bolts of silk from France or England, in colors no one ever saw in these parts. And that one could not get, even in Boston.

I could no longer bear not knowing about William. If, indeed, God was busy elsewhere and did not have time to reveal Himself to the folk of Salem Village, then I would have to satisfy my yearnings by whatever means I could, until He turned His face to us again.

I did not know at that time that the only face I would help bring close to us in Salem, by satisfying my yearnings, was not God's but the Devil's.

2

TITUBA

JOHN INDIAN did not seem surprised to see me. He went right on chopping wood as I approached.

"Wonderin' how long it would be before you came over to visit, little missy," he said.

I hugged my cloak about me. He was a tall man, and I stared. I had never been this close to a blackamoor. I knew they worked in the best houses in Boston. Ships often came into Boston Harbor carrying their human cargo, having first brought rum to the slave traders on the coast of Africa and bartered it for blackamoors. Or sometimes they brought the slaves to the great plantations of the West Indies and traded them for sugar and molasses, which they would then bring home to make into more rum.

"You knew I was out there?" I asked.

"See you all the time." He gave a gentle laugh. "Pondered on when you would walk over. Told Tituba, 'There's a child out there wants in.' Why don't you come with the others, missy?"

"They won't allow it."

"If we waited all our lives to do what was allowed, we would never do anything, now, would we?"

Strange talk for a slave. But he seemed like so much more. His speech was perfect. Surely they weren't all like him. His shirt was bursting its buttons from his exertions, and the gray woolen doublet seemed tight, as if his tawny brown flesh would break free at any moment.

He set aside the ax and picked up a clay pipe. Smoke from the pipe curled over his head as he considered me. I kept my eyes on the bit of bright red fabric that stuck out of his pocket. We didn't see much color in these parts. All frippery in dress was forbidden. And color was frippery.

Why, the whole village was now shunning Bridget Bishop because she had made herself a red bodice.

"Where did you learn to speak the king's English so well?" I asked.

He laughed. "I don't credit the king for it, child. 'Twas my former master taught me. I was born and raised on a plantation in the West Indies. Met my Tituba there."

Yes, I decided, the West Indian place of birth would account for his good diction, his musical manner of speech.

"But my master's luck went bad. We were far up on inland waters, you see. Our overseer, who had dealings with ships' captains, told my master that pirates had plundered many of his cargoes. Truth was, our overseer was in league with the captains, stealing the profits. My master's health went bad. Debts mounted. His wife ran off with the overseer. My master had to sell off his slaves. The Reverend Parris bought me and Tituba."

I absorbed all this in silence.

"You look cold, child. Did you come to see Tituba, now? Or just to stare at me?"

I blushed, for I had been staring in a manner that was most unseemly.

"You have no blackamoors at your house?" he asked.

"My father doesn't abide the slave trade. He refuses to traffic in human souls."

He nodded, while puffing the pipe. "Your father is a good man. Have you no servants?"

"We have fifteen servants."

"Fifteen!" He mused. "Your father must be a wealthy man."

"He brought many from the Isle of Jersey, where his father came from," I explained. "His forebears took refuge there when they fled France. My father brings many servants across the water so they can gain entrance to this land. The men work four years and the women seven, to pay for their passage. Then they are free. May I see Tituba now, please?"

He laughed again. "You want your fortune told? Like the others?"

"I would meet with her," I said. "Would she see me when the others leave? Will they let her speak to me?"

"They do not tell Tituba what to do. No one tells Tituba what to do. I told her it will bring trouble to us all if the reverend finds out about her fortune-telling. She only laughs. Why don't you come into the back passageway, child, and wait? It's much warmer there, and I can smuggle a cup of tea out to you."

I accepted his kind invitation and followed him inside.

Tituba stood in front of the large hearth in the company room, where a crackling fire burned and good things bubbled in pots. She was wearing a bright red turban around her head while she scoured pewter mugs with sand. Skeins of wool were piled in the corner, and a yellow cat dozed at her feet.

With its high, leaded windows and white plastered walls, its rubbed furniture that gleamed in the firelight, the room was a smaller version of our company room at home.

"So you have come to see me at last. Let me take your cloak. It is wet at the edges. Here, sit by the fire."

Gratefully, I sank down near the fire's warmth and accepted a mug of hot cider. She offered me warm corn bread with butter on it. And then, before I knew what she was about, she set a light scarf over my shoulders. Her hands, strong and sure, kneaded the tight muscles at the back of my neck.

I felt completely coddled, and my cares receded. The whole world blurred at the edges as I succumbed to her ministrations.

Yet, inside me, a warning bell went off. Physical pleasure like this went against the Puritan code. In my house, Father hugged my sister and me occasionally, and we always pecked Mama on the cheek before retiring for the night, but affection was not bandied about. Yes, when William came home from a long sea voyage he always hugged me and Mary. And sometimes lifted us right off our feet. But William was boisterous and world-traveled. Therefore, he was forgiven such displays.

But before I could bring myself to resist the touch

of her hands, she moved away. "And why did it take you so long to come, then?"

"The others wouldn't allow me to come with them."

"You asked to join them here, and they said no?"

"Once. I wouldn't ask again. I wouldn't beg."

She sat down and picked up her knitting. "John, set the wood down and leave us, do."

He had come in with an armload of wood, which he set on the side of the hearth. He smiled at us both. "I'll be sweeping the snow from the front doorstep and keeping watch," he said.

She nodded and turned to me. "What is it you want from Tituba?"

I couldn't lie and say I'd simply come to visit. She knew better than that. Apparently everyone who came wanted something from Tituba. I decided to be as plain in my speech as she was.

"I heard that you tell fortunes."

"Tituba only reads what's there in the hand. Tituba tells stories. Tituba makes tea."

"They say you do magic."

Her smile was sad. "Tituba only wakes the magic in the heart."

I had never before heard anyone speak of magic in the heart.

She continued. "These people here in Salem are

harsh. Like the winter when the snows are heavy; they keep winter in their hearts all year round. When Tituba first came to Salem, the Reverend Parris told me why they gave this place that name. Do you know what *Salem* means?"

"No."

" 'City of Peace.' " She frowned. "But there is no peace in this place. There is nothing but hate. The girls who come here hate you because you are of the gentry. Oh yes, Tituba knows this. And the woman who stood out there with you before, in the snow?"

"Goody Bibber?"

"Yes, that is the one. She stands out there often, looking at this place. She, too, would like to join the girls here."

"I didn't know that."

"Tituba knows. They hate Goody Bibber because she is poor and has no man. Tituba never saw such a place for hate as this City of Peace."

"How is it where you come from, Tituba?"

"People hate there, too. But the water is so blue and the sand so white. The coral so pink in the sea. And the birds, oh, they are so brightly colored that you can't tell them from the flowers. And you can't hate long with such beauty around you."

She went on knitting as she spoke. "Tituba gives little Betty Parris that love which her own mama holds back from her. Children are like flowers. Flowers cannot live without sun. Children cannot live without love."

"And the girls who come to see you?"

"Tituba gives them attention they do not get from anyone else. Of course, some of the girls are no longer children. Yet they are not allowed to be women. They are not married. There is no place for them in this way of life here. Except to do hard work or study scriptures. Their hopes and desires die on the vine. This turns them inward. They are seeking ways out of themselves. So they come to Tituba."

"But you do tell fortunes," I said.

"Yes, it brings a little sport into their lives."

"But you are a Christian, Tituba. I see you in Meeting. Surely you know it is sinful."

She gave a little laugh. "Everything is sinful to these people. They think love is a sin. All they speak of is the Devil. Tituba knows that if you speak of the Devil enough he will come 'round."

"Will you tell my fortune?"

"Why do you want Tituba to do this if it is sinful?"

"Because I need to know about my brother, William. He's at sea and we haven't had word of him in two months. I must know if he'll ever come home. I can't bear not knowing anymore, Tituba. I don't care if it is a sin!"

Her smile becalmed me. "You love this brother, William?"

"Oh yes! We all do. And we miss him so."

"Love brought you here to Tituba, then. It won out over this fear of sin. This is good. Let me see your palm."

I showed her my palm. She examined it carefully for a few minutes while she made some murmuring sounds in her throat. Then she shook her head and murmured some more. I thought I would burst with the burden of not knowing.

"Tell me," I begged.

"This William, is he fair of hair and blue of eye?"

"Yes."

"Does he know how to capture the fancy of the ladies?"

I thought of the twinkle in William's eye when he hinted at sojourns in Barbados or France or England. "Yes, yes."

"He will return."

I gasped. "When?"

She clasped her hand over mine and clutched it to her heart. "It is not for Tituba to say when. All is not given for Tituba to see right now."

"Another time?" I asked. "Can I come back another time?"

She paid no heed to my question. "There is another matter," she said.

I knew it! She was keeping something from me! William would come back maimed, with an eye lost or a leg missing. "Tell me."

She stared at me a long time with those brown eyes that had yellow flecks in them. The fire spit and popped. The old cat in the corner got up and stretched, humping her back. I could hear snow falling against the windows, and it seemed as if all the world was closed off. As if there was only this moment, cut out of the rest of the fabric of time and stretched near to tearing. And Tituba, holding my hand against her heart and gazing at me with those brown eyes, while the yellow flecks in them turned to gold.

"When William returns there will be a great outpouring of joy in your family. But there will be great sadness as well."

"What is the reason for this sadness?"

"It is not given for Tituba to know, but it has to do with happenings in this village. Such happenings will touch your family. And the families of many others."

"Does it have to do with our charter?" I asked. "Will Reverend Mather be lost at sea bringing it home to us?"

"It has nothing to do with over there." She gestured with her head to the window, indicating England. "It has to do with this village. You are mindful of all the trouble here now."

"Yes. Just the other day, my father took up his musket and went to help hunt wolves on the edges of this village."

"Child, there is more trouble here now than wolves. It's the people. They would eat one another alive if they could."

I shivered. She was right, of course, but the passion behind those words frightened me. "You don't like it here, do you, Tituba?"

She shook her head no and lowered her eyes.

"Does the Reverend Parris beat you?"

"He is sick of soul. This town is not good to its ministers. One left because of the constant bickering. Another they almost starved out. This one failed as a merchant in the Indies. Being minister here is just a way for him to keep his family, no more."

"The townsfolk didn't want him," I told her. "He wanted to be deeded the parsonage. He wanted thirty cords of wood, cut and stacked for him. He got naught of what he asked for."

"His face is craggy like rocks," she said. "His voice drains the color from this place. Even his little sickly daughter fears him. His niece Abigail has the same sickness of spirit. And I fear it is upon the other children who come here, too. This afternoon a new one came."

I looked up quickly. "Ann Putnam?"

"That is the one. She is only twelve but wise and cruel beyond her years. Her mother taught her well. She sent little Ann to see how she can use Tituba to take revenge on her enemies here in the village."

I paid close heed. This woman was not dull, I minded. She had powers to conjure, yes, but more than that—she could read people's hearts. I must always be forthright in my dealings with her.

"I would come to see you again," I said.

She closed her eyes and breathed deeply. "Yes."

"Will you read my palm and tell me more next time?"

"I will tell you what it is given Tituba to see."

She did not caution me to keep my own good counsel about the visit. No such words were necessary between us. She took the light shawl from my shoulders, helped me on with my cloak, and bade me hasten home quickly. Then she accompanied me to the back door, where John Indian had brought around my horse and cart.

He smiled at me. "I fed the little fellow," he said.

"Thank you, John Indian."

"I brushed the snow from him, also."

I patted Molasses, and then John Indian held out

a carrot for me to give him. "His patience should be rewarded," he said.

I felt becalmed as I drove off, with a peace greater than any I ever got from attending Meeting. I knew I was wrong to feel so, but I also knew that in such troubled times I had to take my peace where I found it.

3

FOUR CREATURES

🌿. THE HOUR WAS
late by the time I got to Salem Town, where candlelight from all the house windows threw a soft glow
out on darkened streets. I knew I was in trouble, for
in the cart I still had many of the items I was supposed
to have distributed to the poor of Salem Village: precious packets of needles and skeins of wool, an iron
cook pot or two, bolts of warm flannel, some molasses,
flour, and salted codfish.

Mama would want to know why I had returned
with my cargo. And so it was that I determined
to lie.

I was not practiced in the art of dissembling, the
word given to such a sin. There had been no need in

my life, up until now, to keep any of my doings from my parents. But in the next few months I was to learn the art of dissembling well.

I knew what I must do, exactly, at that moment. I must ask Jeb, our stable boy with the limp, to keep the cart of goods in the stable until I could dispose of them on another trip tomorrow.

But as fate would have it, I did not have to resort to such deception. For I met four creatures in the snow on the empty streets of Salem Town that evening. And they all helped me.

The first was a rooting pig.

Wandering pigs were a plague in both Salem Town and Salem Village. Frequently they would break out of their pens in the village, where most of them lived, and wander at will into town, where they would then proceed to enjoy the contents of people's gardens.

In winter they came for slops to the back doors of Salem Town's fancy residences and ordinaries. Or to steal the codfish drying on rocks along the shore. It wasn't enough that the people from both the town and the village fought with each other over cattle-grazing rights, property boundaries, and class distinctions; the wandering pigs caused more quarrels than anything.

This particular pig ran right out in front of Molasses, who shied and whinnied in fright. I held the reins taut and shooed the pig, but it wouldn't move. Then a thought came to me.

I got out of the cart, rummaged around in back, and came out with two ears of dried corn. It is excellent for popping when put in an earthenware pot and covered with ashes in the hearth. My father says the Indian Squanto taught Captain Standish and the original settlers to pop corn like this years ago.

The pig took the corn and ran off with it.

The next creature I met was John Dorich. John was sixteen that winter, the age of my sister, Mary. We had all gone to dame school together. John now worked as apprentice to Josiah Green, who was proprietor of the wharf in town. Because he was about the wharf every day, John had learned to swim, manage small boats, salt down fish, barter goods, and fall through the ice and not drown. He often boasted to me of his accomplishments.

Among those accomplishments he also numbered the ability to lie and to run off from his master without being caught. He was also privy to talk that went on between ships' captains and crews, which meant he was one of the first to get news from Boston Harbor.

"What keeps you out at this hour, Susanna?" he asked.

"I was delivering some of Mama's offerings to the poor. And you?"

"I'm looking for adventure."

John's father was middling well-to-do, but his

mother had died a few years after John was born, and his stepmother, having borne his father several more children, had pushed John out of the house before his time. Thus his apprenticeship, since age ten, with Josiah Green.

As with all apprentices, he lived with his master. Beneath all his bravado, John was a troubled lad. Anyone could perceive that. His boasting and bragging only served to cover his real feelings.

"Is your father home this night?" he asked.

"Yes, and probably at meat with the rest of the family this minute. And I'm late," I said dismally.

"Would your father be wont to give a coin of the realm for some information?"

A coin of the realm, indeed! He did have a lively mind. But I must pay him heed. He could have information about ships and such. "What kind of information?"

"If I told you, I wouldn't get a coin from your father."

"Tell me," I insisted. My tardiness would be forgiven if I came into the house with information.

"What would it profit me?"

"I've bolts of flannel."

"I've no need for such."

"Husked corn for popping."

"I can get all of that I want."

"Twists of tobacco."

"Very well, I'll relieve you of some tobacco twists for what I have to say."

"Agreed." And I was down off the seat again to rummage around in the cart. I handed the tobacco twists to him. "Now tell me," I ordered.

"Three ships are riding at anchor in Boston Harbor. Just come in this day. One from Barbados."

My heart jumped inside me. "You know their names?"

"One is the *Spotted Cow*. Another the *Deliverance*, I think. I can't recollect the name of the third."

I could scarcely breathe, my mind was working so fast. Even if the third ship wasn't the *William and Susanna*—and it most likely wasn't or Father would have had word already—the captain of any of the ships might have some news of William.

"Thank you, John," I said.

He nodded. "Have a care, Susanna. You shouldn't be about so late on the streets."

As I drove down English Street toward my father's house, my eyelashes fringed with falling snow, I met the third and fourth creatures:

Sarah Good and her little girl Dorcas. Sarah was the town hag. Lord, forgive me. Those are not my words; they were applied to her by our magistrates after she was accused of spreading smallpox in the most recent epidemic.

It is not in the Puritan soul to be merciful to those

36

who go about as tramps. The Puritan code leaves no room for those who manifest oddities or weaknesses of nature. The Puritan virtues are very plain. They are hard work, cleanliness, orderliness of mind and manner, perseverance, courage, piety, a knowledge of one's sins, a desire for forgiveness, hatred for the Devil and all his works, obedience to the clergy, and impatience with heathens.

Heathens, of course, are Baptists, Quakers, and all other manner of miserable heretics.

Sarah Good embodied everything the proper Puritan was supposed to disdain. She was unkempt in appearance. She smoked a pipe. And while her husband, who was landless, went about hiring himself out as a laborer, Sarah went begging. In the past she had taken all of her many children with her as she went door-to-door asking for handouts. But the town magistrates had seen to it that her children were taken in by various good-standing members of the community.

Somehow she had managed to keep her youngest, five-year-old Dorcas, with her. And now she was again with child.

She nodded to me as I approached. "How are ye this evening?"

"I'm fair to middling, Mistress Good. And you?"

"It's this cough that's a plague to me." And she went into a spasm of coughing.

"You should be home. And little Dorcas with you."

"We haven't finished our rounds yet this night. I've nary enough for the soup pot for when my William comes home from his labors."

I noticed how little Dorcas was shivering in the flimsy cloak that would not suffice once winter came in full force. I minded that bolt of good wool behind me in the cart, as well as the flour and sugar, the salted codfish, and the corn.

Well, Susanna English, I told myself, you've sinned enough for one day. Here is how you can make up for it. If Sarah Good isn't the poor of Salem, no one is.

But in my heart I knew the wrong of such thinking. I knew my mother's wares were not meant for Sarah Good alone. And that I would be violating some code of honor by handing them all over to her just to be done with my chore. But exactly what code of honor would be violated by helping out these miserable creatures, I was not sure.

I was afflicted with confusion. And since this is not a state of mind of which I was very fond, I ended it all by scrambling from my seat and rummaging around again in the cart's depths.

"Here, take this bolt of wool," I said to Sarah. "My mother wants you to have it for a new cloak for Dorcas."

The woman was fully taken back. "She does?"

"Yes. And here, take this salted codfish. And this bag of flour, and go home and bake some bread for your husband."

She accepted my gifts in wonderment. The lines on her face softened. And the wrinkles wreathed a smile.

"I thank ye so much, dear child."

"Go home now," I chided. "The wind blows bitter this night. Get little Dorcas to a warm fire before she catches her death."

I got back into the cart and guided Molasses down the rest of English Street. The cart was much lighter now, for it was empty.

As for my heart, it was lighter, too. But it was also very full of good feeling. I don't care if Mama does scold, I told myself. Giving all those things to Sarah Good was worth it.

4

MY FATHER'S HOUSE

MY FAMILY WAS
indeed at meat when I went into the house. And on
one side of the highly polished three-foot-wide board
that was our table, a place was, as always, set for
William. Mayhap he would come in the door some
night as we took our meal.

"You're late," my father said.

"And wet," Mama added. She was not the kind to
scold, but she took one look at my muddy, soaking
skirts and I knew what she was thinking—that I
would take cold.

"I'm all right, Mama. In truth, all I need is food."
I took my place next to Mary at the board. Like
Mama, Mary was spotlessly dressed in soft wool with

a white collar and apron. But while Mama's dress was gray, Mary's was the color of the sky on a bright June day. I felt ragged beside them.

"Where have you been?" Mary whispered. "Here I've been sewing all afternoon, and you've been out sporting. You sly fox."

I heaped my plate with wild venison stew, corn bread, and boiled clams, then filled a small bowl with sallet herbs. "Stitching your dowry again, no doubt," I teased. "I know you love to dream your way through the afternoon, sister. Is Thomas coming to call?"

She was being courted by Thomas Hitchbourne, son of a well-to-do shipbuilder. Thomas's father was ready to launch a thirty-ton bark to trade for furs along the coast.

"At least he calls," she said, "not like your Johnathan."

"He isn't my Johnathan." But I blushed with pleasure at his name. Johnathan Hathorne, son of our local magistrate, was one of the most promising young men hereabouts. He'd made several calls in the fall, but when he came of an evening to sit in our company room, he was shy to the point of being tongue-tied. I had grown impatient with his shyness and had done little to encourage him. So he hadn't been around in over a fortnight.

"I heard tell he's going to Boston next week when his father hears cases there for the General Court of

41

the colony," she said. "There are pretty girls aplenty in Boston."

"Enough," my father admonished. "I'll have no bickering at this table."

"There's plum cake for delicacy," Mary said, nudging me.

Our table was always graced with such treasures because both my parents were gentry. Nevertheless, they wanted Mary and me always to behave like proper Puritans. They both had their own reasons.

Father had given up an idyllic childhood at age eighteen to run away from the Isle of Jersey and go to sea. He arrived in Salem without a shilling and started as a country peddler. My mother's family, the Hollingsworths, had been Virginia planters visiting up north.

Father happened by where Mama and her family were staying. Mama took pity on him and offered him beer in a silver mug. Her father liked young Phillip's enterprising spirit and lent him money to purchase a ship.

Mama and Father married, and Father's business flourished, but he was ever mindful of his humble beginnings and wanted us to be, also.

As for Mama, she felt guilty because her husband's prosperity came mostly from shipping and trading with foreign countries during war—from the great

Indian War in 1675 to King William's war, which began in 1689 and was still raging in the Mohawk Valley and parts of New England. Father got many contracts from the English navy. So Mama's mind went from enjoying our luxuries to making us do penance for them.

There were times that Mary and I wore silks and laces and we had figs in wine on our table. But we were not to be lulled by such pleasures. For we knew that Monday could be a silk-and-lace day and Tuesday a day of brown linen skirts and bodices.

This was a brown linen day. I saw that as soon as I sat down.

"What kept you, daughter?" Father asked.

"You know how it is in the village," I said. "Everyone pretends disinterest in Salem Town but would keep me there all night catching up on our news."

"Did you deliver all my offerings for the poor?" Mama asked.

She was especially concerned these days about giving to the poor. For she had decided that William's disappearance was God's punishment on us for Father's successes.

"They are all delivered, Mama." It was no lie. They were.

"You missed prayers." Father was eyeing me. A clever merchant, he knew when someone was keeping

43

something from him about a damaged cargo of fancy goods. And he knew when a daughter was holding back the truth.

"I'll make up for it this evening, honored Father."

He grunted and picked up his sterling silver mug of ale, the same mug Mama served him with that day they met so long ago. He took a hearty gulp and set it down. His gaze penetrated my heart.

"I have good news," I said.

"And what would that be?" Father asked.

"Three ships are riding at anchor in Boston Harbor. Just in this day. One from Barbados."

Mother gave a small cry. Father's expression never changed. "From whence this news?"

"From John Dorich."

"Oh, Phillip, you must find out," Mama said. "Seek what word you can, even if it means going to Boston."

Father remained calm. "We have been down this path too often, Mary," he said. "You know false hope is more cruel than despair."

"Can we ignore any hope? No matter how fragile?" Mama asked.

Father sighed. "You know I will pursue the matter, Mary, though my contacts in Boston would have let me know of any word concerning William."

"They are busy men, with their minds on matters of commerce," Mama said. "And after being at sea for months, the captains and crews won't stay around the docks long enough to be questioned."

"I'll go to Boston tomorrow, Mary." Father's voice was filled with patience.

"Thank you, Phillip. And I will say extra prayers. And fast. I'll not wear silk for a year. If only . . ."

"Mary." Father spoke firmly. "William's life is worth more than silk dresses. You know it, I know it, and God knows it. You must stop tormenting yourself. I doubt if wearing rough wool will get William back. God doesn't resort to such bartering. Would that He did!"

Mama's eyes filled with tears. "Reverend Mather advises fasting."

"Cotton Mather is a blockhead," Father said. "Any man who wastes time writing reports on witchcraft hasn't the sense of a gander."

"Phillip!" Mama's face went white. "You financed his father's voyage to England."

"His father is a good man. Cotton is a dunderhead. I've known such since Cotton encouraged that frenzy in the North End of Boston over the antics of that Irish washerwoman they said was a witch. That was almost four years ago now, and still the man hasn't gained a whit of sense. Witches in Boston. I didn't believe it then, and I won't believe it now." He took another gulp of ale. The matter was finished.

"Mister English, sir, there's a woman at the back

45

door who begs a word with you." Deborah, our kitchen maid, came into the room.

"Is she hungry?" Father asked. "Give her some food."

"Not hungry, sir. Says she'll speak with you this night or not leave. She has a child with her, and I fear they're half frozen to death."

"Oh, all right, I'll come." Father got up and left the room.

Alarm spread through me. Mistress Good! At our back door! It could only be she, here to beg for more handouts. I sat frozen, scarcely able to eat, while Mama and Mary chatted about possible news from Boston concerning William.

It seemed an hour before Father returned to his place at the table, but it was truly only about ten minutes. For a moment he just stood there.

"What is it, Phillip?" Mama asked.

"Just Mistress Good, the beggar woman." He was looking at me with a great measure of sadness. "Susanna, I would see you in my library after supper."

"I would tell your mother of your deceit, but it would break her heart. She has enough to break her heart these days."

My father was middling tall and given to plumpness in his mature years. He had kind brown eyes

46

and a pleasant face. His voice made me feel more secure than the town watch making his rounds at night and crying out the hour and telling us "all is well" while I was snug in bed.

My father's presence was benign, not threatening like that of Reverend Parris and some other men. Even when he wore his tall-crowned hat and black cloak, garments that signified authority. But he was angry at that moment. And when he was angry, we always paid heed.

I waited, saying nothing.

"You have not been truthful, Susanna. You did not give your mother's provisions to the poor for whom she intended them. You gave them to Mistress Good."

"But Sarah Good is poor, honored Father. More so than anyone in the village. I considered it an act of charity to give her the provisions."

"Then why did you keep your sudden outpouring of charity from your mother?"

I bowed my head. "Because I knew she wanted her goods spread amongst many."

"How came you to return to town with so much in the cart? What happened in the village?"

"I spent more time than proper there."

"Doing what?"

"Talking."

"With whom?"

"I met some girls walking. Betty Parrish and her cousin Abigail. Elizabeth Booth, Susannah Sheldon."

"Gossiping, you mean. And you know how your mother and I hate gossip. Is that it?"

"Yes, honored Father." Oh, I was quick with my lies, a true daughter of Eve!

"And so then you were late, still with a cart full of items, and you met Mistress Good and pretended to be the benevolent Angel of the Lord, is that it?"

"No, Father, that's not how it was."

"Tell me, then. How was it, daughter?"

I cast my eyes around the room, thinking. I looked to his desk, where his papers and implements for drawing, his journals, and his parchment sketches of ships all sat next to his quill pens and inkhorn in cozy disarray. I loved that room. Richly bound books, some hand stitched, filled the shelves. The sight of all that becalmed me.

"I perceived that Sarah Good was the poorest of the poor, and I didn't think it right to pass her by. She needed everything I gave her."

He waited, puffing his pipe.

I went on. "I cannot abide half the rules, you see."

"What rules?"

"These Puritan ordinances we must live under. I try to be a good Puritan, but I fear I never will be. I cannot see, Father, why a man should sit in the stocks all day for kissing his wife in public. Or why some local Indians are fined for gathering wood on the Sabbath. Or why slanderous speech earns someone a whipping."

I looked into his face. He seemed interested in my views. I went on.

"And I just don't believe, as Reverend Parris preaches, that we are all born depraved. Or sentenced to eternal damnation simply by fact of being alive!"

There! I had put into words what had plagued me for so long, unformed thoughts that took life this night and jumped off my tongue. For the past year such thoughts had confused me, and I'd been afraid to utter them lest they be considered blasphemy. But the events of this night had all conspired to make me speak out.

Father set down his pipe and regarded me with bemused affection. "Daughter, it pleases me that you choose to think for yourself."

"You're not angry with me, then?"

"Enlightened thoughts coming from a child of mine will never bring me to anger. We live in a country yet unexplored. Who knows how large it is beyond our modest settlements? Our young people should have the minds and hearts to match the territory we propose to inhabit."

I felt my spirit lift.

"But, daughter"—and now he frowned—"such

thoughts are best kept within these walls. Our ministers do not realize that God's kingdom here on earth is composed of men and women made of flesh and blood. We are not saints. We complain of heavy taxes from the Crown, yet burden ourselves with principles we have no hope of upholding."

Did all this mean he would forgive me, then?

"I often wonder why our ministers and magistrates don't consider one fact. Which is that the same spirit that brought us here, for whatever diverse reasons, can make us splinter this colony into individual hotbeds of freedom if they suffocate us with their claims of superior holiness."

He opened his arms then, and I went to him. He embraced me. "Think for yourself, daughter. But know when to speak and when to remain silent."

"You aren't angry with me, then?"

He frowned. "I must punish you for lying to your mother." He paced the room, his hands clasped behind his back, thinking. "It was on my mind to bring you to Boston with me tomorrow. But this will be your punishment: now you must stay home."

He knew how I loved Boston. It was truly our City on the Hill, as our colony's founders had called it. Its wharves could accommodate vessels in from far parts of the world. Its twisting streets and lanes were full of interesting people. Bookstores abounded. You could wear your best silks in Boston and not be frowned upon. They had Harvard College, the Common, silversmiths, wharves laden with cargo from distant lands.

I made a sound of protest, but he continued pacing. "Nay, daughter, I must deny myself your company, pleasant though it be. I will go alone. You will stay here. And offer to take another shipment of goods to the poor in the village tomorrow for your mother."

And so it was that I took the cart to Salem Village again the next day. Ellinor was still feeling poorly, so I went alone. The early morning sun was bright, glistening on the surface of the snow. I stopped at all the houses on the list Mama had given me, and I made haste and was done before my appointed time.

And then, early in the afternoon, I went again to see Tituba.

5

BEYOND THE CAULDRON'S
BUBBLING CONTENTS

NOW THAT I look back on that winter of 1691–1692, I understand truths that were frozen to me then as if under the ice in the brooks around Salem. One truth was that I was drawn to the parsonage, to the harsh, wind-scrubbed, and brooding outline it cut against the winter blue sky. In the rear, its sloped lean-to roof was hugged by the silhouettes of trees.

There was something ominous about it, from its weather-beaten shingles—some of which hung half off in a state of disrepair—to the tarnished bronze open-mouthed lion that served as a knocker on the front door. In the winter wind, two shutters on the back window creaked, loose on their hinges. And even the smoke that puffed from its chimneys seemed more halfhearted than lively and inviting. But I was drawn to it, nevertheless; and in the waning afternoon sun, which brought out all its shabbiness, the house beckoned to me like a lost soul.

"So you've returned," Tituba said to me as I entered by the rear passage and came into the company room. Her back was to me. She greeted me without turning. "How have you kept?"

"I'm well," I said. "We thought there might be word of William. My father went to Boston today to investigate three ships just in from sea voyages."

She laughed lightly. "Your father could have saved himself the trouble. It will be a while yet before William returns. Did you tell your father my feelings on the matter?"

"No."

She turned around. Her hands were busy darning a small tear in a child's woolen cape. She kept right on working, not looking at me. "So, you did not tell your people you were here."

"No."

"And why is that?"

"I thought it best not to."

She nodded and seemed pleased. Gesturing for me to sit on a settle bench near the fire, she sat also, after offering me a mug of hot cider.

"Little Betty has come down with malignant

fever," she said. "I have been giving her broth every hour. And special decoctions of root and herb."

"And Abigail?" I asked. "Does she have it, too? They are both so young."

"Young, yes," she agreed. "But the wolves that howl in the night on the edge of town are more innocent." And having said such, she got up to stir a kettle in the hearth.

This announcement discomforted me. It was the first I had heard her say anything uncharitable against Betty and Abigail. Just yesterday she had told me how she gave little Betty the love her mother withheld from her. I sipped my cider. It came to me that all this was leading up to something. What, I did not know. But I would wait and see. As brother William always advised, I would listen more than speak, for in such a manner even a fool can learn.

"You came because you feel matters are unfinished between us," she said.

"Yes."

She smiled. "The sorrow of all humankind is that we can never complete what is between any two people to our satisfaction."

"You had more in the group this morning, didn't you?" I asked. "As I approached, I saw two new members leaving."

"Yes. Gertrude Pope and Elizabeth Hubbard.

The group is forming a new texture now. It is falling into place."

"How is that?" My curiosity bested me. I was determined to pretend disinterest in the group, but the desire to know more about them was a sickness inside me.

"Leaders are coming forth," she said.

"Leaders?"

"Yes. One would think they would be the older girls. But Ann Putnam is the one with the quick mind."

I felt a stirring of jealousy. "She's only twelve."

"She is wise beyond her years, thanks to her mother. She knows about the star called Wormwood. She knows about the depravity of man."

I felt a shiver run through me.

"She knows the Book of Revelation. Her mother has guided her through it. She has read *Day of Doom*. She could be an apt pupil of the Devil himself. The other girls all mind what she says and look to her for guidance. She is here for evil. The others are here for mischief."

"You will teach her no evil."

"Even if I chose to, there is nothing I could teach her. She is beyond my powers."

I was casting around inside myself to respond to this disturbing news when there was a cry from the staircase in the hallway.

"And the Lord sayeth unto Moses, 'Whosoever hath sinned against Me, him will I blot out of My book!' "

The words were almost shrieked, not spoken. I jumped. For there on the stairway, arms outstretched, like an apparition in her woolen nightdress, was little Betty Parris.

Tituba got to her feet instantly. "Child, you should be in bed."

"A sinless newborn infant goes straight to the tortures of Hell without baptism. What hope have we?" The child had glided into the room like one who was sleepwalking. She walked around me, putting the question to me. Her pale face was bright with the luster of fever. Her eyes glistened.

"Would you like to sit by the fire for a while?" Tituba asked.

"I must say the Lord's Prayer," Betty said dreamily. "I must fast."

"No fasting, now," Tituba said. "How about some nice warm broth?"

But the child had fastened her eyes upon me. "He will visit or send His plague among such as are clothed with strange apparel," she said.

"I'm not wearing strange apparel," I said.

"You have worn silks and laces. I have seen you thus garbed. Why come you here?"

"I have come to visit Tituba."

"They will punish you if they find out. The others. Only people they allow can come."

Her voice was hushed, but the words chilled me. "I am here of my own free will," I said steadfastly.

"We tamper with the forbidden here. God's work is not conducted in this house. There are mysteries in this company room that go beyond the cauldron's bubbling contents."

"I tamper with nothing."

"You are not wanted here. The others don't want you. They know your father is an outlander, not decently born in England but on the Isle of Jersey."

I glared at her. "Who tells you this?"

"They know that he has a papist name. Your name is not English. It suffered a 'sea change' on his voyage to America. Isn't that right?"

"I wouldn't believe everything Ann Putnam says if I were you, Betty Parris."

"Your father's name was L'Anglois. He has papist leanings," she accused.

Everyone knew that a person with even the flimsiest connections to the Catholic faith was as much a heretic as a Quaker or a Baptist.

Over Betty's head, Tituba made a sign to me, shaking her own head and scowling. I kept my silence.

"God broods on Salem," the child went on. "My father says in his pulpit that God has reason to brood on us. Men can be kept from murder but not from hate. From adultery but not from lust. From theft but not from greed. We are all sinners in Salem."

"I am sure your father does not think you a sinner, Betty," I said.

She looked at me as if I had not understood a word, as if I were dimwitted. "There is no mercy from God for those He has destined to damnation." Her tone was quiet, as if she were remarking on the weather.

"I'm sorry you are ill, Betty," I told her kindly. "I had no intent to disturb you."

"It is my spirit that is disturbed. 'Tis the Lord's judgment for my sins. My good father preaches against certain pleasures. I indulge in them."

"We all disobey our parents on occasion."

She raised her fever-bright eyes to me. "You disobey more than your father, coming here. When the others find out, your spirit will be afflicted, too."

"They won't find out," I said.

She rewarded me with a sly smile. "But they must, don't you see? 'Tis my bounden duty to tell them."

"Why?"

"I know not why," she said dismally. "But I heed their call before I heed God's. Before I heed my father's. Oh, God!" And she screamed shrilly again and commenced to weep. "Why do I have these unhallowed needs?"

I became truly frightened then, but Tituba calmly

took her in hand and led her back into the hall and up the stairs. "I will be down in a moment," she said. "But you should take your leave soon."

I waited by the fire in the silent room. In a very short while, Tituba crept back down the stairway, cautioning me with a finger to her mouth to speak in whispers.

"What ails her?" I asked.

She took up her darning. "The fever."

But I sensed it was more, sensed that Tituba was keeping things from me. That in all little Betty's delirium, she had spoken the truth. That, indeed, what was going on in this house was not God's work.

But if not God's work in a parsonage, then whose?

I shuddered. "Will she tell the others I was here?" I asked Tituba.

" 'Twas the fever speaking," she assured me. "By tomorrow she will remember nothing of what she said. Or about your being here. She dips in and out of these spells."

"Spells?"

"She is a delicate child. What the others take in sport, she takes seriously."

I was starting to understand. "You mean your little sorceries?"

"Yes. They trouble her. 'Tis only an innocent game, but the guilt weighs heavily on her mind. She is filled with Puritan righteousness."

"Then why do you do it?"

"Because they ask it of me," she said simply. "Oh, child, go, go. And keep an innocent heart. No one will believe anything Betty says. They are all sensible of her sickly condition. Tomorrow all will be well and forgotten."

I went. But not without misgiving. Betty's tongue had discomforted me. There had been some appeal in her cries, some warning in her ravings that I could not discount or put down to fever. By the time I reached home that day I was convinced that little Betty Parris had been right. There *were* mysteries in the Parris household that went beyond the cauldron's bubbling contents.

And given the prospect of the dreary winter ahead, the drudgery of routine—even in our house, where my mother and father were more tolerant of innocent laughter, occasional song, and book reading, as well as entertaining of friends—I knew that I would be drawn back to the Parris household to find out what those mysteries were.

When I would return, I did not know. But I would go back. For there was still the possibility that Tituba would give me more word about William.

6

THE GIRL WHO LIVED
IN THE WOODS

LEADEN SKIES
hung heavy with snow the night Father returned from
Boston. Gusty winds blew from the northeast. He
had no word of William. The *Amity* had come into
Boston Harbor from Barbados with nails, ironware,
fancy goods, and hogsheads of sugar and molasses.
Yes, its captain had heard of the *William and Susanna*,
but that ship had left Barbados before he arrived.

He had heard that its intrepid captain was eluding
some Spanish pirates, headed perhaps for the Christo-
pher Islands. Or Grenada or Guadeloupe.

The night Father returned, we went into the company room after our meal, sitting in front of the fire
to hear his latest news from Boston. Mary and I were

stitching hems on linen pillow covers when Deborah answered the thumping sound at our front door and admitted Deliverance and William Hobbs from Topsfield Village.

"What brings you out on such a night?" Father asked.

As soon as they were in front of our hearth, partaking of Canary wine and honey cakes, William Hobbs told his tale.

"Our daughter has run off again. She has not been home in two nights." William Hobbs choked back a sob. Deliverance leaned her head on Mama's shoulder.

All of Salem knew of the Hobbses' troubles. Their only child, Abigail, who was sixteen, insisted on living in the woods.

She preferred sleeping outdoors with the creatures of the wild to sleeping under her parents' roof. She could live for days in the salt marshes and the forests, existing on nature's bounty, and never look the worse for it.

"She took some provisions," William Hobbs said. "And she will drink from streams. In summer, my wife and I abide such behavior, difficult as it is. But these nights are so cold! And snow is coming!"

Clearly the poor man was beside himself. Deliverance could not even speak; she just kept shaking her head and sniffing.

"We can no longer bear it," William Hobbs admitted. "We have done all in our power to make a proper and God-fearing young woman of her. She refuses to go to Meeting. She reads books! Not the Bible! Books! She writes her thoughts down on parchment. Surely this is not proper behavior for a young woman."

"My own daughters read," Father said.

The poor man was bewildered. "More than the Bible?"

Father's voice was calm. "They have access to all the works in my library. Susanna just finished reading *Paradise Lost*."

The man turned to regard me as if I had just sprouted horns. "Do they prefer the company of geese and deer to that of their mother and father? Do they slip about on the salt marshes or follow the streams like Indian women?"

"Thank the Lord, they give us no torments," Father said.

William Hobbs set his mug aside. "We have already been warned by the selectmen and magistrates. They say if we cannot keep our daughter from roaming the woods like an Indian squaw, they will take her from us and place her with some family who can."

Father got up from his chair and began to pace. "I have always been of the mind that people's affairs are their own," he said. "But that is an Anglican belief. The Puritan community sees people's private affairs as belonging to the community. You will want to find your daughter before the authorities do."

"She has been seen in Salem Village. In the vicinity of the parsonage," William Hobbs said.

My heart leapt inside me. Dear Lord, had Abigail Hobbs heard of the circle? Was she wanting to belong? Mary and I had gone to dame school with her. Even then she had been unruly and wild, fearing nobody.

I knew what concerned our magistrates and why the Hobbses were so fearful for Abigail.

Women who read books, who wrote their thoughts on parchment, did not honor their fathers or ministers. They were considered dangerous. It went back to the time of Anne Hutchinson.

Father had told us about Anne. She had been a self-proclaimed minister who had put forth her own independent religious beliefs and argued against ordained ministers.

Massachusetts Bay Colony had never quite recovered from the heresies of Anne Hutchinson. In 1637, its leaders had tried her for thinking on her own and banished her and her followers to Rhode Island.

"I will send some servants out tomorrow to search for your daughter," Father said.

"She will run from your servants," William Hobbs predicted. "She is as nimble as a fox."

"What would you have me do, then?" Father asked.

"Your own daughters know her from dame school. Perhaps they could seek her out and ask her to come home."

"I'll go, Father," I volunteered immediately. I did not want Mary near the parsonage, asking questions about what was going on. "Abigail never liked Mary. Don't you remember, Mary, how she would take your hornbook in school? And how she would hide it from you?"

"Yes," Mary said. "Forgive me, Mistress Hobbs, but she was a scourge to everyone."

"I think little of being the mother of such a dafter," Deliverance admitted.

"I'll go with Ellinor, Father," I said.

The snow held back overnight, thank the Lord. But all of nature seemed intent upon making us miserable. The air the next morning was so damp that one's bones near froze. Molasses's breath came out in spurts of whiteness, as did our own.

Before we got to the parsonage, I dispatched Ellinor to the house of Joseph Putnam, uncle of Ann. His wife, Elizabeth, had just given birth, and I sent Ellinor along with a basket of honey cakes and sweetmeats from our pantry.

With her out of the way, I approached the parsonage. Abigail sat on some evergreen branches on the ground, a bit away from the house.

"Abigail?"

"We are here on the edge of madness, Susanna English. We are a lost people without a home."

"You have a home, Abigail. And parents who wish you there."

"Don't you ever think that we sit on the edge of a vast wilderness, without knowing what's out there?" She looked up at me intently.

"I try not to ponder that, Abigail."

"My father says we are a special people who have a covenant with God. I say God has forgotten us, if He ever knew we exist."

I was not about to debate the Lord's concern for us in such raw surroundings. "Aren't you cold?" I asked.

"It is nothing as to the coldness in some people's hearts."

"Abigail, we don't see each other much anymore. But I always felt in sympathy with you, even back in dame school."

"You were one of the kinder ones," she admitted. "But I hated dame school. I longed to read poetry. They made us read the Bible. Didn't you ever wonder why the evergreen stays green all winter while all the other trees die? Why the mockingbird mocks those different from him? Where the geese go in winter?"

"The geese go south. My mother's family lives in Virginia. I've been there. My father's ships go there regularly to trade."

"I'd like to see Virginia." Abigail drew up her knees, bundled her cloak around her, and gazed pensively into the winter landscape. "Wouldn't you love to go to London?"

"Someday, my brother William will take me with him on a real sea voyage," I said. "And I'll meet a fine ship's captain. William will introduce me to him. And we'll marry, and my husband will take me with him on his travels. We'll winter in the West Indies. I'll travel to London and come home wearing the latest fashions."

"And they'll persecute you here in Salem for wearing such clothing. I hate this whole place. I hate the rules they make us live under. I care not for fine clothing, but they won't even let us read books. All our elders are hypocrites."

"Surely not your good people. Or mine, Abigail."

"Most grown-ups are. Living as I do, I see and cannot be seen. Outside people's houses at night, I hear their sobbing, their cries, their voices raised in argument. One summer's evening, I came upon two people in the wood. They were naked and frolicking.

He was married to someone else and so was she. Next day, I saw them in Meeting with their rightful spouses. I don't go to Meeting anymore. Have they sent you to fetch me home, Susanna?"

"Your mother and father have much concern for you."

"They know I can care for myself."

"The magistrates have threatened your mother and father, saying they will put you with another family if yours cannot keep you properly."

"I could live on my own. This rule Puritans have about making unmarried people live under the guidance of a family is senseless."

"Such talk will bring you trouble, Abigail. You've heard the stories about Anne Hutchinson."

"Yes, and my only regret is that she lived before my time. I do harm to no one. Why do the magistrates plague me?"

"They want you to be a true daughter to your parents."

"I've helped my father slaughter his hogs. I've sheared sheep, washed and bleached and dyed wool, hoed the garden, helped with the candle and soap making. What I do with my own time is my affair."

"They say you are acting like an Indian squaw."

She sighed. "I wish I could be as free as an Indian squaw." She stood up. "It isn't my wandering ways that upset the magistrates. It's that I read. And write down my thoughts. So, now I am to go home and be a docile daughter? And what of my needs? My wants?"

"What is it that you want, Abigail?" I asked.

"To be free. To be away from Salem. Or if I must stay here, to find someone who can show me how to give voice to my thoughts and needs, no matter how different I am. Why must we all be cut from the same cloth?"

"It's the way of things," I said.

"Well, it's the wrong way. And the magistrates and ministers may fool themselves into believing that everyone is falling in with their way of thinking. But I could tell them what I see late at night when no one knows I am looking. Most people I observe are as discontented as I."

She gathered her things. Then, as we turned to my horse and cart, she put a hand on my arm and pointed to the parsonage. "There's a place I could tell them about. The sounds that come from inside that house could be from Hell."

"What have you heard, Abigail?"

"Our good reverend beats his woman slave. His daughter screeches like a wildcat at night. And a covey of girls has been going in and out there every day. All gaggling like geese. Something is amiss in that house."

"Perhaps the girls go in to study Scripture. It is, after all, a parsonage."

She laughed. "The girls come only when the reverend and his wife are out. I've watched the beavers, chipmunks, squirrels, raccoons, and foxes long enough to know when creatures are in disharmony with nature."

'We're not the ones to pass judgment, Abigail."

"I know what I've seen," she insisted.

As we went toward the cart, the back door of the parsonage banged open and someone called our names. Ann Putnam was hurrying across the frozen ground. "Wait," she pleaded.

Breathless from her exertions, she stood before us. "You've both been hovering about here spying, haven't you?"

I was taken aback by the pinched look in her face, her pallor, the tightness about her mouth that gave her the look of a grown woman.

"What is there to spy on?" Abigail asked.

"Don't evade my question," Ann said.

"We're measuring the boundaries of this property," Abigail told her. "That should interest you, Ann. Your mother has spent her life involved in property disputes."

"I'd have a care if I were you, Abigail Hobbs," the girl warned. "The town fathers are growing weary of your heathen ways."

"Does Reverend Parris know you girls come here

every day when he and his wife are out?" Abigail asked.

"We come for spiritual advice."

"From John Indian? Or Tituba?" Abigail's laugh rang out in the cold.

"We wait for the reverend," Ann said.

"Then why do you leave before he comes home? I care not for what you do in there," Abigail said. "But don't mix in my affairs, or the good reverend will soon know something is amiss in his house."

Ann turned to me. "She doesn't concern me. No one would listen to the ravings of a woman who lives in the woods at night. But you do concern me, Susanna English. Betty Parris has told me of your visits. I ask you not to come again."

"I don't need an invitation to visit the parsonage," I said.

"You are not welcome," she said. Her manner brooked no argument. Her voice was strong, her demeanor unflinching. There was about her some purpose that could not be denied. But I was nobody's fool.

"I'd be more concerned with little Betty Parris," I told her. "Whatever goes on in there is causing her great torment."

"She had malignant fever. She is better now."

But I caught the gleam of wariness in her eye. And

I knew I'd touched on some truth. When she spoke again, her voice was tempered.

"We cannot have people here if we cannot trust them," she explained quietly. "So don't hover about, please."

"I've better places to hover," Abigail said. "Come along, Susanna; leave the little coven of witches to themselves."

"What mean you by that?" Ann Putnam screamed.

We turned to see her shivering in the cold. "No harm," Abigail said. "Why are you afraid?"

"I'm not afraid."

"I know fear in one of God's creatures, be it a deer in the woods or a person."

"The accusation of witchcraft is not to be taken lightly," Ann said.

Again Abigail laughed. "All girls 'twixt twelve and twenty are witches, don't you know that? How else can we accomplish our goal of becoming women?"

I saw Ann breathe easier. "Leave us alone. And we'll leave you alone, Abigail Hobbs. You have your pleasures, and we have ours. In this godforsaken place, we must find our pleasures where we can."

"What pleasures do you find in there?" I asked.

"Our gatherings are too simple for the likes of you, Susanna English," she said. "We're plain village girls whiling away the long and lonely hours. We have never worn silks and laces. We don't have books or fancy things in our houses. Your presence would give us great discomfort."

"Keep your precious gathering," Abigail said. "Come along, Susanna."

We took our leave. "She always was the queer one," Abigail said, setting her things in my cart. "Her mother made her such. So, Miss Sly Wench, you have been inside. How else would you know that what they do disturbs little Betty?"

"I met Betty one afternoon and she told me," I lied. "The poor child was frightened to death. She'd escaped the house and was walking around out here. I thought her ravings were from the fever."

I don't know if Abigail believed me. We spoke no more of the matter, and then when we picked up Ellinor we discussed other things. But I'd had a profitable afternoon, for I came away convinced something sinister was going on in the parsonage. Why else would Ann Putnam have ordered us away?

I'd learned, too, that I was not the only one dissatisfied with our way of life in Salem. Abigail Hobbs was trying to escape its suffocating effects. And, if I were to be truly honest with myself, so were the girls in the circle.

7

THE EVIL HAND

WINTER CAME
in earnest to Salem. Streams froze. The wind and
the wolves howled at night. People stayed by their
firesides. Midwinter in New England is a frightful
time when people take sick and die, a time of frozen
whiteness divided only by night and day.

The snows were deep, and people ventured out just
to care for their livestock, to fetch firewood, to clear
paths to go to Meeting. Melancholy gripped many.

Christmas came and went. Celebration was forbidden in Massachusetts Bay Colony, declared papist and
pagan at the same time. But in our house my parents
remembered Christmas celebrations of their child-
hoods, and so we had plum cake, sugared treats,

roast pig and fowl, and every other kind of delicacy Deborah and Mama could concoct in our kitchen.

One day, Elizabeth Putnam, wife of Joseph, came to Mama's variety shop. It was her first trip out after giving birth.

"It is said that little Betty Parris is having hysterical fits," Elizabeth said as she stood examining a red kersey bed cover.

"Is it the fever?" Mama asked.

"No, it is more like a turning of the mind. She cries in her sleep, will not eat, screams words at her parents. She says their slave Tituba is trying to poison her. She sees objects flying at her from across the room. She sometimes does not know her father when he picks her up."

"He is a harsh man, but everyone knows of his love for that child," Mama said.

"She has thrown the Bible across the room."

"Winter afflicts the spirit," Mama said.

" 'Tis more than winter."

"What, then?" Mama asked.

"Her cousin Abigail is also afflicted. The good reverend has tried to keep his troubles to himself, but with so many coming and going at the parsonage, secrets cannot long be kept."

"Has he summoned the doctor?" Mama inquired.

"He has."

"And?"

"The doctor has dismissed all ailments but one," Elizabeth Putnam said. "He has pronounced the evil hand to be on them."

Mama's round, pleasant face stopped smiling. "What mean you by that?" she asked.

" 'Tis not my meaning but that of Doctor Griggs."

"What means he, then?"

"Witchcraft."

Mama's eyes sought mine. Bright sunlight streamed in the shop's window. Outside we could see people tramping about in the snow. A dog barked. A child's laughter echoed.

"Nonsense," Mama said briskly.

"So my husband, Joseph, says. He distrusts the verdict. As do many others. Those who have seen the girls say they look none the worse when they come out of their fits. And why should they? Tituba makes her little charges every delicacy to eat. They have been excused from prayers, study, from every chore. They have thrown off the yoke of discipline and do things other children would be whipped for."

"You sound as if you don't believe it, then," Mama said.

"Neither Joseph nor I believe it. Reverend Parris insists it is true. That those in demoniac possession throw off all discipline. So now he has sought the aid of other ministers. They will soon come and pray over the girls."

"My husband and I do not hold with witchcraft," Mama said.

Elizabeth Putnam's face broke into a smile. She nodded happily at Mama and then at me. "I am glad to know that, Mary. Now, tell me, what is the price of the bed cover? My husband is so happy with the birth of our daughter, Mary, he would have me select a gift for myself."

"It is one pound, ten shillings," Mama said. "It comes from England."

" 'Tis beautiful. But such a sum would buy ten bushels of wheat."

Mama smiled. " 'Tis my experience that when a husband wishes to buy his wife a gift, she would be a fool to refuse it."

"I will tell Joseph he may purchase this bed cover for me. Mary, don't spread this about, but I heard talk today of other girls now being afflicted."

"Who?" Mama asked.

"Mary Walcott. Elizabeth Booth. Susannah Sheldon. And Ann Putnam, my husband's niece."

I felt the color drain from my face. All were members of the circle!

Elizabeth Putnam picked up her basket and patted Mama's hand. "We must keep our senses, my Joseph says, and not give in to hysteria. Good day to you, Mary. Good day, Susanna."

Mama and I stared at each other for a moment,

then Mama shook her head and went back to work. I was stocking items on the shelves, but I could not concentrate.

Witchcraft? The evil hand on Betty and Abigail and Ann Putnam? Likely the girls' afflictions had more to do with the mischief going on in the circle. I sensed young Ann Putnam's work in all of this. What path was she leading them down, I wondered.

It was plain that Reverend Parris did not know what transpired under his roof, or he would be meting out punishment, stern man that he was, and not calling in other ministers to pray over the girls. Yes, that was it! I stood as if under a spell myself, staring at the bolts of linsey-woolsey, buckram, and flannel, the rows of clogs, and the men's doublets on the shelves in front of me. And the thought came to me, like the sun through the window.

Little Betty was tormented with fear of her father discovering their doings. Perhaps he had already discovered what they were about. And to throw a mantle of protection over themselves, the other girls were mimicking Betty's condition.

Oh! I turned so quickly that I knocked a bottle from a shelf. It crashed to the floor.

"Susanna!" Mama's hand flew to her breast. "You startled me."

"I'm sorry, Mama." I picked up the unbroken

bottle. Should I step forth and tell what manner of games were going on in the parsonage? No, no, I should try to speak with one of the girls first, to determine if they were lying, because I was the only one outside their circle who had reason to suspect them of it.

"Mama, wouldn't it be charitable if I brought some fresh apple tarts to Ann Putnam's? Of all those afflicted girls, she lives closest to us. Perhaps I could help her."

"Ann Putnam and her mother are trouble," Mama said grimly. "Sometimes I find it difficult to believe that Joseph Putnam is related to his brother, husband of the elder Ann. That woman has devoted her life to making others miserable. And her husband has allowed it. I don't know what's afflicting the daughter, but I'll wager the mother's had a hand in it."

"Then Ann is ill-used by her mother and deserves our sympathy," I argued.

"I have no sympathy for anyone in that household."

"Mama, it isn't like you to be uncharitable."

"Ann Putnam, senior, is just like her older sister who went before her," Mama explained. "You don't remember Mary Bayley. She was married to the first minister in Salem. She went on having child after child. They all died at birth. Mary Bayley blamed her malcontent neighbors because they hectored her husband. For some reason, this town has a way of doing such to its ministers. She blamed them for killing her children."

Mama sighed. "Ann Putnam, senior, still blames people hereabouts for her sister's death. As well as for the babes she herself lost before she had little Ann."

"I didn't know she had children before Ann."

"A number. All dead. Like her older sister's. Instead of thanking the Lord she has Ann, she's made the child into a miniature of herself. Taught that child to blame everyone else for their woes. I tell you, I'll have naught to do with those people."

It was one of the most passionate outbursts I'd ever heard from my mother. Why, she was red in the face when she was finished. I'd never seen her that agitated, even when she spoke of William.

"Besides," she said, "I don't want you afflicted."

"But you and Father don't hold with witchcraft," I reminded her. "Being afflicted by witches isn't catching. Is it, Mama?"

She smiled at me. "Very well, I'll ask your father when we sup tonight. We'll see what he says."

"What do I say?" Father spooned his soup into his mouth and cut a generous slice of cheese for himself. "I think, daughter, that I hate the very suggestion of witchcraft. I see it as the Puritan mind at its worst."

He paused to spoon in more soup. "Four years

ago they hung that poor Goody Glover on Boston Common. She was no more a witch than I am. Her only fault was she was a poor Irish washerwoman."

He eyed me across the table. Mary and I sat open-mouthed. "The Reverend Parris was living in Boston with his family at the time. He attended the hanging. Took the little girls to see it. No wonder those poor children are now daft. Go, child; take your apple tarts and your smiling face, and go visit Ann Putnam. But with one request."

I waited.

"Wait until the ministers pray over the girls. Let the holy men do their praying, lest they think I sent you to interfere with their fight against the Devil. And say nothing to Ann Putnam about witchcraft. Be your own happy self. Perhaps you can help her as you helped Abigail Hobbs."

And so I went. And became part of the madness that had come to Salem. I went, but I never told my parents what it was that I discovered.

8

APPLE TARTS AND CONVERSATION

⟩⟩ MERCY LEWIS, maidservant to the Putnams, let me in to their main hall and took my cloak while Ann Putnam and her mother stood by.

Mercy said nothing by way of greeting, though I felt her eyes upon me and saw her exchange sly glances with young Ann. Mrs. Putnam was a forbidding-looking woman, tall and big of bone with a sallow face. For a few very uncomfortable minutes, I sensed they all knew why I had come. They must have discussed me at length after my last meeting with Ann, when she told me not to come back to the parsonage.

"Let's take your lovely apple tarts and go into the company room," young Ann said sweetly. "Mercy, do bring us some hot cider. Mama, Susanna English and I have much in the way of young girls' talk to occupy us. We would like our privacy."

Why did this make me feel that the girl's mother consented only because she trusted Ann to deal with me as I deserved? I don't know. But there was some undercurrent of understanding between this mother and daughter that had more to do with evil than with love. I was sensible of that immediately. It was as if these two moved together through dark and swirling waters toward some whirlpool they could not avoid. And would not think of avoiding.

In the company room, before the fire, Ann startled me with her forthrightness. As soon as the door closed, all traces of sweetness left. She did not even bid me to sit, but stood before me, fists clenched as she spoke.

"I was expecting you. If you have come to make trouble, be aware you are uncovering a hornets' nest. You will be sorry."

"What trouble could I make for you, Ann?" I tried to remain calm, but I was frightened. I was not welcome. Something unpleasant was about to happen between us, yet I did not know the nature of it.

"I know exactly what I have gotten myself into," she said. "But you do not. So be warned. If you came to probe for my secrets, you may not be happy with what you learn here this day."

"Ann, I came to appeal to you."

"For what? I suppose you wish to cast your lot in with us more, now that we have so much attention."

"I wanted to join your circle before, Ann. But I no longer harbor such a wish. I came to ask you to speak out before it is too late."

"Speak out about what?" she inquired innocently.

"Ann, please let there be no deceit between us," I begged. "I wish you no harm. Nor any of the other girls in the circle. But the doctor's verdict about the evil hand being on Abigail Williams and little Betty Parris is not true. We both know such. Someone must speak out now, before the matter is out of hand."

Her fists unclenched, and she turned away from me. "It is already out of hand," she said.

I moved quickly to stand before her. "What mean you by that?"

She laughed. It was a cruel and heartless laugh. "The ministers prayed over us. You should have seen them. They hovered over us like old crows. We couldn't look each other in the eyes for fear of giggling. Of course, that Reverend Noyes from Salem Town is young and a bachelor and rather dashing. I thought I would swoon when he put his hands on me."

I was, indeed, taken aback by this. And I could not keep my feelings from showing in my face. "Ann, the laying on of hands is holy!"

Again, she laughed. "You wouldn't think such, from the gleam in his eye."

"Ann, you're only twelve," I said.

"But far from a child. Or so people will soon find out."

Her manner conveyed a threat.

"Ann, what mean you by that?"

She started swaying in a little skipping dance around the room. She picked up her skirts and held them out gracefully. She closed her eyes and hummed a tune. When at last she answered, a cold chill went through me.

"The ministers wish us to name our tormentors."

I gasped. "Ann! You cannot do that! There are no tormentors!"

She continued her dancing moves, smiling at me. "We must do it. They want us to name people. This whole town wants it." She stopped dancing and considered me solemnly. "There is so much evil in this town." She sighed. "All my life I have heard of it from my mother. No one knows what she and her sister endured here. And we are plagued by so many other troubles. The elders are looking for someone to blame. We will give them many someones."

"You will give forth the names of people as witches? When you know you girls are not really afflicted?"

"We will, and the elders will be glad to know that

the cause of the bickering and trouble in this place lies not at their own feet but is the fault of witches living amongst us."

I understood now. "Is that why you joined the circle?" I asked. "To use it to avenge your mother's enemies?"

She became angry. Her face twisted into bitter lines. "Yes, my mother sent me! Because she has disturbing dreams of her dead sister and her children. They stretch their hands out to her and implore her for help. My mother doesn't know what they want from her. She sent me to Tituba to contact her dead sister."

"I am sorry for your mother's sorrows," I said. "Did Tituba help her?"

"She was about to. She was in a trance one day, when little Betty Parris got frightened. . . . The child is a dafter. She ruined everything. I warned her about those fits. She wanted to go to her father and tell him what we were about. I told her that if she exposed our sport, her father would have her whipped in public and sent out to live with another family."

So that was it! No surprise, then, that little Betty was so terrified. "Her father would never do that," I said.

"I needed to keep her quiet."

"And so she became more terrified."

"She became uncontrollable."

I was utterly taken aback by this young girl's lack of heart. Indeed, she had no heart. "And that was when her father called the doctor?"

"She needed a whipping, not a doctor. But then something else happened. The reverend and his wife started to coddle Betty. Abigail got jealous of the attention lavished on her cousin and got the fits, too."

"So then the rest of you claimed the same affliction," I said dully, still not believing what I was hearing.

"We had to. Don't you understand? Why let Betty and Abigail have all the sport? They were the center of attention. The other girls and I discussed it. We decided this was our chance to take part in something very wondrous."

"Wondrous?" I could not abide what I was hearing.

"Yes! It was our chance to break out of the chains they bind us with in this dreary place. But also, we couldn't abandon Abigail and Betty. They didn't have the sense to carry this matter through and not be discovered. They needed our advice. So we met with them and told them that they must outwit the elders or we would all be terribly punished. We swore fidelity to one another."

"And will keep that fidelity?"

"There is no going back now. The die is cast. We are bound together, and we will stay together and give succor to each other until the end."

Until the end. The words sounded so dreadful. "So you will continue to deceive, then, though innocent people be named as your tormentors."

"Don't trouble your head about it, Susanna English. There are people in this town who are far from innocent, who deserve whatever befalls them."

"And you consider yourself capable of judging who those people might be?"

She faced me, unflinching. She raised her pointed chin. Her eyes glittered. "I am familiar with the history of Salem. I know who the troublemakers are."

"You mean your mother will tell you. And they will all be her enemies. You will be her tool, Ann."

Her face became flushed. She started to tremble. "Only troublemakers, outcasts, and malcontents will be named. We do this place a favor! It is no concern of yours, Susanna English. Why don't you go back to your fancy house with all the gables and not meddle in matters you don't understand?"

"I understand all I need to," I said. "I wish to God I did not understand."

Once again her smile took on an evil quality. "I hope you don't intend to break charity with us and tell what we are about. You wouldn't do that, would you, Susanna English?"

Now it was my turn to tremble. For what I was facing in this young girl was evil, pure and simple. I had heard of evil all my life, in Meeting, from ministers. I had heard people speak of it in casual terms. But never before I stood in that room that day with Ann Putnam did I feel its presence. I did then, and it was terrible to behold.

"I think you will not tell what you know," she said quietly. "For if you do, we will cry out on your parents."

"Cry out?" I asked.

"Let me put it plain, Susanna English. We will name them as witches."

"Everyone will then know you for a grievous liar!" I shouted.

Her laughter pealed. "We can name anyone. The power has been given to us by the ministers themselves. They anxiously look to us for the names. In a fortnight, we will be questioned again in the Parris study. I think you will not tell, Susanna English."

"God forgive you!"

"Hold your tongue! Or your household will be touched."

I could not believe this was happening. I looked around me, around the well-appointed company room that so resembled ours at home, a room that bespoke the solid dedication to God and family and place that was at the heart of all Puritan belief. And I knew in my bones, in that moment, that what went on in these sturdy walls would soon disrupt our whole way of life in Salem.

And I was powerless to do anything about it. I felt myself go limp with fear. "I must go now," I said to Ann Putnam.

"Do go. And remember what I said this day. And thank you for the apple tarts."

Her evil laughter followed me out of the room.

9

CHOOSING SIDES

HER EVIL LAUGH-
ter stayed with me. I heard it at night in my dreams.
But I told no one of what had transpired. For I had
no doubt that if I did, Ann Putnam would bring
trouble down on my family.

If she proved to be anything like her mother, she
was not a person to be dallied with. I did not wish to
find out.

So I did not betray her. But her disclosures troubled me greatly. So I worked harder at chores, helping Mama more and more in her shop. Partly to
redeem myself for the sin of keeping such knowledge
from my parents and partly to hear what news neighbors brought in.

Joseph Putnam came in one day to purchase the red kersey bed cover. I had always liked Joseph Putnam. He was tall and amiable, a fine-looking man with a face that had both a sober strength and a boyish eagerness.

"How is the new babe?" Mama inquired.

"Thriving."

Mama wrapped the bed cover and tied the bundle for him. He thanked her solemnly. "Words should be let go with due consideration, Mary," he said.

Mama nodded and waited.

"I know you and your husband to be people of common sense. In the near future, we people of like mind will have to support each other."

"Is there trouble, Joseph?" Mama was never one to shilly-shally about things.

"I feel the hysteria connected with this witch business will get worse before it abates. It is fed on distrust in our community, on old quarrels between neighbors."

"Then it is well fed before it starts," Mama said.

"It has started, Mary. Reverend Parris caught Tituba making a witch cake. He was so enraged, he beat her."

"Why would Tituba do such a thing?" Mama asked.

"It is an old custom where she comes from. She

told the reverend she hoped to conjure forth the witches before people could be named. But we heard she was encouraged to make it by Mary Sibley, aunt of Mary Walcott, one of the afflicted girls."

"For what reason?" Mama asked.

"Mayhap to raise suspicions of witchcraft against Tituba."

I was standing in a corner of the shop. Upon hearing this, I uttered a gasp of surprise. But no one heeded me, thank Heaven.

"Mary, it is good to know there are enlightened people hereabouts to consult with as matters worsen." And so saying, Joseph Putnam nodded to me and started for the door. "In the days ahead, it will surprise us all to see who amongst us falls in with the hysteria and who holds himself above it. Or uses it for personal advantage."

"Who would do such a thing as to take personal gain from the troubles of others?" Mama wondered aloud.

"In times of crisis," Joseph Putnam said, "there are always those to use misfortune for personal gain. That will be the real evil we see in Salem. Not some girls trembling in fits. And I say this though my own niece be one of them."

"I pray for your niece, Joseph," Mama said.

"Thank you, Mary." He nodded at me and left.

Two days later, Elizabeth Porter came into the shop. She was sister to Magistrate John Hathorne and wife to Israel Porter. Joseph Putnam was her son-in-law; his wife, Elizabeth, her daughter.

"Reverend Deodat Lawson returned to Salem Village and his former parish yesterday," she told Mama. "He witnessed the fits of the girls. He said the violence that overcame them was well beyond the power of the ordinary person."

"He has come all the way from Boston to study our problem?" Mama asked.

"Yes. And he put up at Ingersoll's Ordinary. There he saw Mary Walcott in one of her fits. He said the poor girl acted as if a witch was biting her."

"What was that child doing at Ingersoll's Ordinary?" Mama asked.

"Performing, Mary. The afflicted girls have taken to going to Ingersoll's so people can witness their torments. Mr. Ingersoll's tavern has picked up considerably in business."

"Shameful," Mama said.

"I take it then, Mary, that you and your husband do not subscribe to the theory of witchcraft?"

"We do not!" Mama said firmly. "We never have. But I fear we will soon be in the minority."

Elizabeth nodded. "We who believe in kind must give comfort to each other and consult often," she said. Then she smiled at me. "Have you seen my young nephew Johnathan Hathorne lately?"

"I haven't," I answered.

"He is much taken with you. Are you sensible of that, Susanna?"

"No, ma'am." It was the only modest and seemly answer I could give. "He hasn't been around to call."

"He's been to Boston with his father." She turned back to Mama. "My brother will be one of the magistrates to hear the cases if this witch business comes to trial."

"Do you think it will come to such?" Mama asked.

"It will. My brother and Magistrate Corwin are thinking of accepting any mischief that follows quarrels between neighbors as grounds for suspicion of guilt of witchcraft."

Mama and I just stared at the woman.

"I don't agree with my brother on that point. There have been too many quarrels in Salem between neighbors."

No one said anything for a moment as we considered this.

"Does my nephew capture your fancy, Susanna?" she asked.

"He's a handsome lad," I admitted. "And quick of mind."

"He'll be off to Harvard next year. But he needs a push with the fairer sex. I'll speak with him."

Before I could tell her not to trouble herself, she was off. Mama and I looked at each other and laughed. Then I felt the need for air. Too many thoughts were crowding my mind. So I put my cloak on and walked through town in the sunshine, heading toward the wharf.

It was a bright day with a brisk breeze. The flags of two countries, Holland and France, were snapping on the masts of two trading vessels bobbing at anchor in the harbor. Likely their captains were delivering needles, nails, and gunpowder for hides, dried beef, salted fish, and whale oil.

I loved the wharf. Two of my father's shallops were waiting for the outgoing tide so they could carry wheat to Boston. I stood there, a solitary figure apart from the activity, breathing in the fresh salt air. I'd hoped to find my father, but he was nowhere in sight.

"Ho! Susanna!"

John Dorich came out of the countinghouse on the end of the wharf. "Some sport!" He laughed. "Have you heard the news?"

"About what?"

"What indeed? The only subject on everyone's tongue these days."

"You mean the cold weather?"

"I mean the afflicted girls. You take my meaning, Susanna English. Why pretend otherwise?"

"I'm done to death by the subject."

"You've livelier subjects to discuss?"

"I don't consider the matter lively. I consider it dull."

"Then you don't wish to hear the news?"

"Stop plaguing me, John. What is it? Or do you want a coin of the realm for your news?"

"My, we're contentious today, aren't we?"

"It's just that I'm weary of hearing about the antics of a few girls who have all of Salem in a state of anxiety."

"Do I sense jealousy for the attention they are receiving? You must admit that no one our age ever got such attention before."

His brown eyes were merry yet full of wisdom. John always had been a calculating soul. I could see he was not taking the antics of the girls seriously, and that cheered me. He was wise enough, perhaps, to see it all for what it was. Nonetheless, I must be careful in my conversation, I decided, and not give away what I knew.

"Reverend Lawson visited the parsonage and found Abigail running through the rooms, flapping her arms like a bat, upsetting household objects, and wrestling with a creature that wasn't there," he told me.

"A sad business," I said.

"I say it's the greatest sport we've seen hereabouts for years."

"What meaning am I to take from that, John?"

He moved closer. His voice dropped to a whisper. "Would that I were of the fairer sex. I'd be one of their number."

"John! What a thing to say!"

"And why not? Consider it, Susanna. I think they carry on so for sport; that they are done to death with life hereabouts. And with the rules. And with sitting for hours in Meeting hearing Reverend Parris tell us how we're all damned. I think they have decided to become comic oddities."

"How terrible to think such," I said.

" 'Tis wondrous. A few young girls have their elders running to their Bibles and searching Scripture. At the same time, they have managed to throw off all restrictions. I think they are a bunch of jackanapes who are teasing—and enjoying the distress of their elders."

He sought my eyes. His own were steady and unblinking. "That can't be possible, John," I said. "They've been declared possessed by learned men."

"Yes, and ever since then they've been having a wonderful time of it. Are you going to the parsonage tomorrow? The girls will name their tormentors."

"My family is not much taken with this witchcraft business."

"Ha! Your father will be there as a town elder. I'm going. Can I fetch you?"

"Thank you, John, no. I haven't decided if I should go."

"Well, I wouldn't miss it."

"Be careful of your tongue, John. You can't confide such views to just anyone. Most people don't know you as I do."

He smiled sadly. "Do you know me, Susanna?"

"Since dame school."

"But who knows another? Reverend Parris doesn't know his own daughter at this time."

"What are you saying now, John?"

"Why should the girls have all the sport? Can't young men be possessed by witches, too?"

"John!"

"These girls will be known throughout the colony before this is over. They will hold sway over learned men. Well, I'm bound to have some of that power, Susanna. I'm weary of working hard and being passed over as nothing."

I had no reply for that. He walked off, whistling, down the wharf. Poor John, I thought. He must be lonely and friendless indeed, if he seeks such a goal.

What had our way of life done to us, that to escape it some would resort to feigning possession by the dark consorts of eternity? While others would rush to believe them? And still others would rush to join them for their own advantage?

I went home thinking that everyone in Salem was most likely choosing sides in the witchcraft business, the same as John Dorich. I felt sad, for the community was torn apart already by old quarrels, and now it would be even more disrupted.

10

NAMING THE TORMENTORS

◤. AT BREAKFAST
the next day, Father told us he was going to the
parsonage.

"I have informed the ministers and magistrates
that I hold no belief in witchcraft," he said. "I suggested that Salem would do better to put its energies
into planning the spring crops, increasing our trade,
and improving the quality of our dame schools."

"What did they reply to that?" Mama asked.

"That they wanted my presence, along with the
presence of many other good people, in the place
where they would pray to God that the girls be relieved of their torments. I could not say no to such a
request."

" 'Tis a reasonable request to a reasonable man," Mama said.

"May I go with you, honored Father?" I asked.

"Why would you wish to, child?"

"I know so many of the afflicted."

"Do you go as a curiosity seeker or as a seeker of truth?"

"To know the truth, Father." It was no lie. Perhaps this day the truth would be known at the parsonage.

He nodded. "I must depart immediately. If you accompany me, mind your demeanor. This is a sad day for Salem, not a country fair as so many are making it out to be."

The front of the parsonage property was crowded with wagons and carriages, people on horseback, and little groups of folks conversing in the cold as if they were at a September corn husking.

" 'Tis as I thought, a country fair," Father said as we alighted from the carriage. "Daughter, with the press of people, you may not be able to get inside. I hesitate leaving you here in the cold."

"I'll keep, Father."

But he called out to the first familiar and trustworthy face. "Here! Johnathan Hathorne!"

"Sir?" Johnathan approached and took off his hat.

I minded he seemed two inches taller than when we last met.

"Johnathan, would you escort Susanna inside, if possible? Find a quiet place in the midst of the madness and deliver her to me afterward?"

"I'd be happy to, sir. How are you, Susanna?"

"Hello, Johnathan." Oh, why had his aunt Elizabeth said he was taken with me? How could I face him now? I was tongue-tied. And then someone opened the front door of the parsonage and everyone started to move toward it. I felt Johnathan's strong hand under my elbow, guiding me, felt him staring down at me.

"I've been meaning to call, Susanna. All winter."

I looked up at him. The sun brought out light streaks in his curly brown hair. His face was ruddy from the cold, and I noticed how broad his shoulders were under the cloak, how his cheekbones were prominent and strong, his eyes so blue. The nose was a bit pronounced, but I sensed his face would grow in strength to do it justice.

"It's just that every time I intended to come 'round, something else happened. First I went with my father to Boston. Other times I had to be man about the house, in his absence, after all this started. He's been very busy conferring with Magistrate Corwin. They have been ransacking their Bibles to find the true meaning of witchcraft."

"Have they found it?" I asked.

"All they've determined is that an accused witch has no right of counsel. All the Bible says is, 'Thou shalt not allow a witch to live.' "

I started to shiver.

"Don't be frightened, Susanna." He paused to look down at me. "None of this will touch you. My father and the other learned men will keep it from spreading."

"I wish I could be sure of that, Johnathan."

For a moment or two we stared at each other, as if we'd just met. When next we looked around, everyone was in the house and the front door was closed.

Johnathan sighed. "We'll never get inside now."

"Yes, we will. Come." And I took his hand. "I'll get us in the back way."

John Indian let us in the back door, and when Johnathan asked how I came to know the man I lied and said I came here on missions of mercy for Mama when little Betty took sick.

We took our cloaks off in the kitchen and stood in its doorway. We could see into the company room, where everyone was assembled.

Before the hearth, at a long table, sat Reverend Nicholas Noyes from Salem Town, Reverend Parris, and Reverend John Hale from Beverly, along with Magistrates Hathorne and Corwin. Joseph Putnam was on a bench to the side with my father. Flanking the other side of the long table were the elder Ann Putnam and her husband. Then someone announced the girls.

They came in single file. A general murmur went through the room. Young Ann Putnam, Mercy Lewis, Mary Warren, Gertrude Pope, Susannah Sheldon, Mary Walcott, and Elizabeth Booth. Betty and Abigail were already seated but soon got to their feet to stand with the others before the elders.

In the silence one could hear the fire crackle. A gust of wind rattled a casement window. Sun shone in on the polished furniture and pewter candlesticks and danced off the white plaster walls. The scene was not unpleasant. But what followed decidedly was.

Reverend Parris spoke. "Tell us, if you can, who has afflicted you thus."

The girls remained silent. He repeated the question, now directing it to Ann Putnam.

"I am not afflicted, Reverend," she said softly. "I am well."

In the next moment it was as if a hurricane broke loose. For Ann Putnam let out a bloodcurdling scream worthy of an attacking Indian. At the same time she hurled herself onto the floor, and her body writhed in jerking movements.

The room came alive as people cried out. "Silence!" Reverend Parris ordered.

He knelt over Ann to hold her quiet. Her thrashing subsided. Still holding her, he prayed quietly. Then he asked again, "Child, who does this to you?"

There came no answer. She seemed to be in a trance. Reverend Parris lifted her limp body and turned to the other girls. "Tell us," his voice boomed, "who is responsible for this evil?"

The girls just stared at him, their eyes blank and glassy.

Reverend Parris then placed Ann Putnam in her mother's lap. He turned to the girls. He was an imposing figure indeed in his black doublet and hose and breeches and his white collar.

"Someone amongst us is in league with the Devil," he said. "If only we knew who it was. You girls must help us. We will protect you, have no fear. We will guard you night and day if necessary. Tell and you will save your whole village from doom. For one person may, with the help of the Devil, destroy a whole town!"

The girls stood, straight and unseeing. Ann Putnam had come to her senses by now. I saw her uncle Joseph Putnam watching her and frowning. He never took his eyes from her. Several times he seemed about to speak, then held back.

Again Reverend Parris turned to Ann. "Who has come to you through this veil of darkness? Speak, child."

Ann slipped off her mother's lap. "I cannot be certain, but there were times I thought I saw a shape."

A murmur of heightened interest from the spectators. Reverend Parris held up his hand for silence. "Can you name the person whose shape it was?"

"I do not wish," Ann said sweetly, "to injure an innocent person's reputation."

And, oh, the anger flowed through me like a river then. I wanted to run into the room and scream out to all of them that she was lying and what she had told me. I made a move in the kitchen doorway, a gesture of helplessness. And Ann Putnam saw me. She turned slightly and looked across heads to me, just long enough to smile, then she turned away.

But in that smile was all the evil that could exist in God's good sunlight. I felt the energy of it directed at me. And I fell back in silence and in fear.

"We will pray now," Reverend Parris said. "We will pray that God gives these poor, suffering girls the strength to know their tormentors."

There was a shuffling movement as everyone knelt on the hard floor. I felt Johnathan's hand on my wrist, pulling me down.

"O great Lord God," Reverend Parris's voice boomed, "look down on this congregation of sinners. See not our sins but our eternal faith in Your mercy! Smite the unrepentant amongst us with Your just anger, but do not visit that anger on these innocents.

Send forth lightenings with rain, but do not turn away from Thy annointed. Behold our plight. Be mindful of our covenant with Thee. We dwell together here in unity to serve Thee. Do not let the scepter of the ungodly abide with the righteous. Do well, O God, unto those amongst us who are true of heart. Move these young ones to name the evil ones who persecute them. Amen."

The whole congregation murmured, "Amen." And just as that was done, Ann Putnam shrieked and threw herself at Reverend Parris.

"They ride on sticks!" she screamed. "They ride on sticks!"

Joseph Putnam was on his feet instantly to seize his niece and hold her firm. I thought I saw him give her a good shake, but I could not be sure of it.

"Who?" Reverend Parris knelt in front of her while her uncle held her firm. "Who rides on sticks? Tell us!"

From a corner by the fireplace, where she had taken refuge in a chair, his own daughter, little Betty, came to her feet and walked toward him as if in a dream.

"Tituba," she said in that frail voice. "It is Tituba who torments us."

One after another, the afflicted girls picked up the name and chanted it. "Tituba, yes, Tituba."

Reverend Parris raised his hands over his head.

"Dear God, have I then housed the Devil's helper under my own roof?"

"It is not only Tituba." Mercy Lewis broke the silence that followed. "Others are with her. I can see them."

"Who? Name the others." Reverend Parris turned to Mercy and pulled her to him. "Name them now and save this town from ruin!"

Mercy exchanged glances with the other girls, who nodded to her. "Sarah Good!" Mercy shouted. "Sarah Osbourne! Tituba!"

The din that followed quickly became an uproar in the room as all the girls took up the chorus and, raising their arms over their heads, danced around Reverend Parris, chanting, "Sarah Good, Sarah Osbourne, Tituba!"

This continued for about three minutes. Johnathan Hathorne and I just stared at each other. I felt my face go white, my knees go weak. "Johnathan, take me out of here," I said.

Outside, in the brightness of midday, I saw the flash of a red bird on a nearby bush, felt the cold air on my face, saw the blue sky. I was surprised to see the world was still the same, that the trees hadn't become uprooted in the uproar and the snow hadn't turned to black mush.

"You're trembling," Johnathan said.

I looked up into his handsome, ruddy face. "There was evil in that room, Johnathan. I could feel it."

"The elders will root it out. They will issue warrants now for the arrest of the witches."

"Arrest?" I stared at him as if he'd taken leave of his senses. "Arrest Tituba? Why, she is only a poor slave who took good care of her charges."

"She was practicing the black arts."

Words of defense for Tituba died on my lips. I could not speak for her without revealing what I knew. "Sarah Good? They've named her because her husband is landless and she wanders the town begging. She has no means, no one to stand up for her."

"She has been named," he said.

"Sarah Osbourne? What of her?"

"My father said she has been under suspicion for a while. She never goes to Meeting. She took William Osbourne into her home and lived with him before marriage, thereby committing offenses against decency."

I could not believe these words of accusation were coming out of Johnathan! "Have you been so influenced by your father?" I asked. "Sarah and William Osbourne are now married. She doesn't go to Meeting because she is bedridden!"

He took my hands into his own. "Susanna, don't let this upset you. Let the matter be dealt with by learned men. You yourself said you felt the evil in that room."

"The evil I felt, Johnathan, was the crying out on innocent people."

"They will be given a chance to prove their innocence."

"You've said the magistrates will not give them rights to counsel. Johnathan, do you believe in witchcraft?"

The whole idea was unthinkable to me. And my whole being filled with fear as I awaited his answer.

"Yes," he said solemnly. "Witches make covenant with the Devil instead of with God. They are set amongst us to do the Devil's bidding."

"And you believe that we now have witches amongst us in Salem?"

"Yes, Susanna. Why else would everyone be here today in this gathering?"

My senses reeled from his admission. How could he believe such? He was so quick of mind, so strong of purpose. I started to cry. He tried to comfort me as we walked around the house. We went to sit in my carriage and wait for Father. He tucked the bed rug around me and spoke of other matters. But I would not be comforted. Something terrible had happened this day in Salem; some darkness worse than night had been released upon us. And I alone knew the truth and could bring light into that darkness.

But I had to protect my family, so I could not speak out.

People were coming out of the parsonage in ones and twos. I caught murmurs of conversation as they went by.

"What has happened?" Johnathan asked one of them.

"Haven't you heard? Hello, Susanna."

I took my hands from my face, and there was John Dorich. "The magistrates are in there issuing warrants for the arrests of the three named witches. I told you, didn't I, Susanna? Those girls have power now!" And he ran off.

"What does he mean by that?" Johnathan asked.

"Nothing. He's just as addle-brained by this as all the rest of you."

"I do not consider myself addle-brained, Susanna."

"You believe in witches," I accused. "And I don't. This is all hysteria, and men of goodwill should stop it."

"They are trying," he insisted. "I'm sorry you are so upset, Susanna. I'm sorry I can't please you and say I don't believe in witches."

"Believe as you wish!" I snapped.

He climbed down from the carriage. "May I come to call?"

I could not answer. How could I bear having him

around, prattling about his father trying the accused witches? "I don't much care," I said finally.

"Well, there is no merit in that answer. I'll give you time, Susanna. I'll be too busy, mayhap, helping my father."

"I'm sure you will be."

"Good day and keep well, Susanna." With that tender parting, he was gone. I sat there lonely and miserable and cold, watching the people come out of the parsonage. They were pausing to huddle in small groups, loath to let go of the excitement.

"Hello, Susanna English."

Abigail Hobbs was coming toward the carriage. "I didn't see you inside," she said. "Isn't this a lark? I came to see what could shock these good folk more than my staying out in the woods at night. I must confess, I'm a little jealous."

"Of what, Abigail?"

"I feel as if I've been shunted aside like stale fish. Nobody will care a fig about my actions after this."

"Don't be silly, Abigail. It's all confusion and mayhem."

"I love confusion and mayhem. I do what I do to raise eyebrows. I take pride in upsetting the town elders. Now I see I'm going to have to resort to additional methods to keep my reputation."

"Abigail, stop talking nonsense."

"You're such a little dove, Susanna. What do you

know, living in that grand house with so many servants and going on trips to Boston with your father? The rest of us young people hereabouts must find our sport where we may."

I stared at her in disbelief. So, then, Abigail Hobbs, too, had simply been trying to break the dreariness of our way of life by her antics. What other revelations was I to become privy to? And how could I bear any more?

"Oh, have you heard?" she asked. "They'll be examining the accused witches tomorrow! And I hear Reverend Parris had Tituba confined to the cow shed."

Tituba! I had completely forgotten to ask John Indian where she was and how she was keeping. Oh, how could I have been so heartless! Tituba, yes, that was it. I must find Tituba.

I looked around and saw Father off with some men, deep in conversation. He would be a while yet. So I slipped out of the carriage, past Abigail, and ran around the side of the parsonage, careful to keep out of sight.

I must get to see Tituba. I must convince her to tell what she knew. Only Tituba could save us now.

11

TITUBA'S TALE

SHE LOOKED
at me through one good eye. The other was swollen
closed. In the corner of the cow shed, Tituba sat on
some clean straw covered with a blanket. Another
blanket was drawn around her hunched shoulders.
The shed was closed and dim, and John Indian held
a lantern.

"Tituba, is this what the good reverend did to
you?" I asked.

For a moment she did not recognize me, then I
saw an intelligent light in her eye. "Ah," she said,
"the little girl from the house with all the gables."

"Oh, Tituba, how cruel of him. How can I ever
go to Meeting and hear him preach again?"

"Not the first time he does such a thing," she said.

"Tituba, I haven't much time. I must speak with you."

She shook her head. "Too much talk. Tituba says it is now time for silence."

"No, Tituba, it is time to speak out! The girls in the circle have named you as one of their tormentors. The magistrates have issued a warrant for your arrest."

She thought this amusing. "They know where Tituba is. Tituba can't go away from this place."

"They'll want to examine you tomorrow. When they do, you must tell them of the secret meetings and what went on in them. So they know the girls are not tormented by witches."

"Tituba already tell."

"You told them of the circle?"

"Tituba say she been meddling in the black arts."

I could not believe this! "Why?" I gasped. I turned to John Indian and asked it of him. He shook his head and did not answer. "Why have you done this, Tituba?" I asked again.

"It is what the reverend wanted to hear. When I told him such, he stop beating Tituba."

"Oh, dear God!" I murmured. Then an idea came to me. "Tituba, tomorrow you can tell the truth to the magistrates."

"Tituba want no more beatings."

"They won't beat you."

"Tituba's master will, if Tituba tell truth. He don't want it known his little daughter and niece are lying."

"Does he know they are lying?"

"He never think this. He know only that Tituba make disaster. He want to believe Tituba is to blame. Others need to think so, also. So Tituba will give them what they need to know."

So she had perceived that Reverend Parris and the others needed someone to blame for Salem's quarrels and troubles.

"They will put you in prison, Tituba."

"Tituba already in prison. Where they put me, the reverend can't beat me no more."

"Can't you convince her to tell the truth tomorrow?" I asked John Indian.

"There be no justice for the likes of us, little missy," he said.

I saw there was no hope here. "Tituba." I took her hand. It was feverish and bruised. "I am your friend, Tituba," I said.

She smiled and closed her eye and leaned her head against the wall. "Things will get bad," she said. "Matters will worsen. I will not be here when it happens, so I tell now. It will get very dark in Salem. Bad winds will blow and take many from this place. Listen to Tituba now."

"I'm listening."

"One night, when it is very dark, you will see, from your street, a ship in the harbor."

My heart beat very fast. "William?"

"No. The ship will not be in the water. It will be in the sky."

In the sky? She must be silly with fever, I decided.

Her good eye opened, and she looked to the opposite wall and raised her free hand to describe what she saw. "A ship made of dark clouds. You will see it against the sky. It will fly the skull and crossbones."

"A pirate ship!"

"Yes. And while you stand there and behold this vision, the shape of the flag will change before your eyes to be like a flag on your father's ship."

"An English flag."

"Yes. Then the ship will disappear. When this happens, brother William will soon be home."

"Oh, Tituba, thank you!"

"Tell no one this."

"I won't. But, oh, please, give thought to what I say! Tell the truth!"

"The air is black over Salem Town," she said. "The sun is gone from this place. Death is in the air. Tituba will do what she must to live. Go now, child. Be brave, don't be foolish. The secret is to know when to speak and when to remain silent. Some never learn this. Those who learn live to an old age."

I shivered. A gust of wind rattled around the corner of the shed. Tituba pushed me from her and turned her face away. Tears streamed down my face as I went out into the cold.

I went home and became sick. That night the cold set in to freeze the heart of the most brave. When morning came, silver with frost on the windowpanes, bitter with bone-numbing cold, I had a quinsy throat and fever. My head was throbbing.

Sickness is nothing to dally with in New England in wintertime, and Mama set about at once applying her remedies, which included hot broth and herbal and root medicine. Nonetheless, before the day was over I could not even raise my head from the pillow.

As the silver whiteness of the days blended one into another as February progressed, I knew what it truly meant to be sick in spirit and body, for I was not only aching and feverish, but miserable of heart over the turn of events in Salem.

My family kept me informed about what was going on with the witch testimony. I insisted upon knowing.

Tituba had confessed to being a witch. For three days, her confession went on in Salem Village Meetinghouse. She told the crowd that gathered of large red and black cats that came to her and bade her serve them. She told of a black dog that ordered her to hurt the afflicted girls.

She recounted how she had ridden on a pole through the blackest of nights with Sarah Osbourne and Sarah Good. She spoke of winged animals with the heads of women. And a little yellow bird that accompanied her on special missions of evil.

She described a tall white-haired man who dressed in black and led a coven of witches in and about the colony of Massachusetts, especially in Essex County. And she told them how she had signed her name in the Devil's book to please this man. And that there were more witches in Salem than just she and Osbourne and Good. But she did not know their names.

Then she admitted that the spectral shapes went into people's homes to torment them. She told the people of Salem what they wanted to hear.

The afflicted girls, sitting in court, too, groaned and threw themselves on the floor, crying and screaming, while Tituba testified. Meanwhile, Osbourne and Good claimed innocence. But no one believed them.

On March 7, when I was still in bed, the two Sarahs were taken to jail in Boston with Tituba.

My sickness persisted. I woke at night with fits of coughing, so I had to be propped up against pillows to breathe. I thought of Tituba in prison. I knew I had lost a good and true friend. I also knew she had taken what truth had been in Salem with her. Except for the truth that was in me. And I was not sure, in my fevered state, what was truth anymore and what wasn't.

12

MAMA TAKES A STAND

🌿 MARY CAME
in from the cold one day, fresh from market. Mama
and I had been sitting by the fire in the company
room. It was March 19. I shall never forget that
day. It was one of my first out of bed and I was
cosseted in a bed rug, sipping tea. Mama was doing
needlework.

"Did you get the lemons and limes?" Mama asked.

A ship was just in at harbor with a large shipment
of fruit, and Mama wanted fresh lemon juice for my
tea. She had promised to make us a lemon cake, for
we were hungry for the taste of these treasures.

"Yes," Mary said. "And you will never guess what
I heard at market."

"Come sit and have tea and tell us," Mama invited. "Is there news of William?"

"Not of William, no. But news. Mistress Parris has sent little Betty away from the village to live here in Salem Town in the home of Stephen Sewall."

"That is good news," Mama agreed. "No child should live in the Parris household."

"There is more," Mary said. "Abigail Williams has accused Rebecca Nurse of witchcraft."

Mama's teacup clanked down rudely in the saucer. "Rebecca Nurse? Never! She is seventy-one, the town matriarch! Why, if the word *goodwife* applies to anyone, it applies to her."

Mary sank down by the warm fire, served herself tea, and nodded. "She is the last person one would think would be named."

Rebecca Nurse was staunch of spirit, kind of heart, learned in Scripture, the mother of four sons and four daughters. She kept a spotless house and a flax garden. She and her husband lived in the old Townsend Bishop house, which was always bustling with the comings and goings of family.

"Not only that," Mary added, "but Ann Putnam, the younger, has accused Martha Cory."

"Martha Cory has been skeptical about this witchcraft business from the beginning," Mama said. We could see she was upset by this news, but she becalmed herself and picked up her needlework again. "Martha

123

goes constantly to Meeting. The woman is no more a witch than I am. Her only trouble is that she talks too much."

"A warrant was sworn today for her arrest," Mary said gloomily.

"But I thought we were finished with accusations, now that they named the three and put them in jail," I said.

We all sat and stared at each other. The March wind rattled against the leaded windows. The fire crackled cheerily.

"To give this conversation a good turn, I met Johnathan Hathorne at market today," Mary said, smiling.

"You give it no good turn," I said gloomily. "His father will send all these dear friends of ours to jail."

"Johnathan inquired after your health," Mary persisted. "I said you would soon be well. He said he would come to call."

"I won't know what to say to him," I admitted.

"To be fair, the son is not the father," Mama reminded me.

"He's more like his father than I'd want him to be."

"Then be mindful of what you say," Mama cautioned. "Say naught of this witchcraft business."

"Does anyone in Salem speak of anything else?" I asked.

Johnathan came to call on the first Lord's Day in April, the third. I was not well enough yet to go to Meeting, and truth to tell I didn't want to go and hear Reverend Parris tell us how sinful we all were. I had lost all faith in the man. But Mary and Mama had gone thither. Father was in his library, studying or praying or doing whatever it was he did when the weather was too raw to row across the bay to St. Michael's.

Deborah took Johnathan's cloak and served him some claret and cakes. He kissed my hand, then presented me with a book beautifully bound in red leather. *The Pilgrim's Progress.*

He brought the outside world in with him, in the color in his face, the wood-smoke fragrance on his clothes. Seeing his broad shoulders and strong wrists and hands, his wind-tousled hair, I felt truly alive.

"I have missed you, Susanna."

I had missed him, too, I realized, seeing him standing before me. I was tongue-tied.

"I have thought of you often and prayed for your recovery."

"Thank you, Johnathan," I said politely.

He sipped his claret and nibbled at the cakes. He spoke of sundry matters, but there was a deadness in the air after those first few words, as if we were both mindful of our distressed last parting.

Finally he set down his mug. "You mustn't bear me ill will because of what my father is doing, Susanna."

"You agree with everything he does," I reminded him.

"I don't. I am here today to tell you I have had doubts."

I stared at him as if he'd taken leave of his senses. "About what?"

"This whole business is foul. I was in court the day they examined Rebecca Nurse. She is a dear woman. She shines with an inner light."

"It will serve her well in prison."

"Ann Putnam, the elder, accused Rebecca of murder. She said her dead sister's children had come to her in a dream in their winding-sheets, telling her that Rebecca murdered them."

"The Putnams are evil, Johnathan. All but Joseph and his wife, Elizabeth. When will you become sensible of this?"

"Elizabeth Putnam is my cousin. I am sensible of it. And much more. My father said in court that an innocent woman would weep before charges of murder. He counted Rebecca a witch because witches cannot shed tears."

Johnathan rested his elbows on his knees and put his head in his hands. "That same day the afflicted girls named Elizabeth Proctor. People go from court to Ingersoll's Ordinary like the whole business is a traveling carnival. At Ingersoll's they fill up on rum and cider and gossip about who will be named next."

"How terrible," I said.

"The afflicted girls go there and have fits. John Indian joins them."

"John Indian?"

"He rolls on the floor. He guides newcomers who come to gawk at the girls through the history of the outbreak of witchcraft in Salem. He boasts that his wife is a witch."

John Indian? I could not believe it. He must be acting so to avoid being cried out on, I thought. Like Tituba, he must have decided that the only way open to him was to give the people what they wanted. "Who named Elizabeth Proctor?" I asked.

"All the girls. Her husband, John, announced one day at Ingersoll's that he'd cured his maidservant, Mary Warren, of her fits by setting her down at her spinning wheel and threatening her with a whipping. But the magistrates sent for her to come to court to testify. After that, the girls cried out on Proctor's wife. Proctor defended his wife in court. But his voice was lost in the screams of the girls. The magistrates believe the girls, not him."

"And you? What do you believe, Johnathan?"

"I started having doubts about the whole witchcraft business after Rebecca Nurse was accused. I went to talk to Joseph Putnam. His sentiments are like a fresh wind. The man keeps his head. I'm so glad my cousin Elizabeth married him and he is near kin. Joseph went to his brother's wife and warned the elder Ann that if she dared touch anyone in his household with her foul lies, she would answer for it."

"Bless him!"

"I honor my father, Susanna. But I tremble to see him denouncing our friends and neighbors. We'll not have a friend left when this business is done. I told him so, and we argued fiercely. I am afraid a rift is coming between us that will never heal."

"I can't do anything about the rift between you and your father, Johnathan," I said. "But you'll have me for a friend. Always."

He blushed and reached out to touch my hand. Had I spoken rashly? Was he strong enough to go against his father and not be swayed in his opinions? Could he be trusted?

I did not know. I only knew that he needed my friendship at that moment, and I gave it.

Just then the front door opened roughly and, in the midst of much clatter, Mama and Mary came into the hall. I saw immediately that Mama was distraught. Mary was trying to soothe her.

"That poor woman," Mama was saying. "What was I supposed to do? Let her sit there alone?"

"You did the right thing, Mama," Mary was saying.

"I sealed my own fate, Mary. Did you hear them? I am now a friend of witches! Oh—" She turned, startled. "Oh, I didn't know we had company."

I ran to her. "Mama, what's happened? Why are you home early from Meeting?"

"Some Meeting." She handed her cloak and shawl to Deborah. "I will have tea, Deborah. Good and strong. Where is my husband?"

"In the library, ma'am. Shall I fetch him?" Deborah asked.

"No, give the man his peace. How are you, Johnathan?"

"I'm well, ma'am. Is there some trouble? Can I be of help?"

Mama sank into a chair by the fire. I could see she was wary of Johnathan's presence, mindful of speaking out in front of him. She shook her head no.

"Mama." I knelt before her. "Johnathan and his father have had a terrible fight over the witchcraft business. Johnathan has come to our way of thinking. You may speak in front of him."

Mama raised her eyes. "What convinced you to have a change of heart, young man?"

"I was in court the day they examined Rebecca Nurse. My father and I have been arguing ever since.

I think he is ready to disown me as a son," Johnathan said miserably.

"Well, you may come here for comfort, then, since I miss my own son." Mama accepted tea from Deborah and waited until she left the room. Then she spoke.

"I never thought I would see such a day in Salem. Sarah Cloyce came to Meeting. You know she is sister to Rebecca Nurse. This is Sacrament Sunday. Sarah was in sore need of solace, since her sister has been named a witch. And what did our congregation do? They shunned her!"

"Oh, Mama, how terrible," I said.

"They moved away from her and left her alone in her pew. I could not bear it, so I bade Mary stay in our pew and went to sit beside her. I held her hand. She was trembling. And what text did Reverend Parris read?"

Johnathan and I waited. Mama raised her blue eyes. They had tears in them. "He read, 'Have I not chosen you twelve and one of you is the Devil?' Well, Sarah begged me to take her out of there. So we left."

"I left, too," Mary said proudly.

"As the door was closing," Mama continued, "I heard Reverend Parris say, 'Christ knows how many devils there are in His church and who they are.' Well, I shall never go back to Salem Meeting again, I can tell you."

"Nor I," Mary announced.

" 'Friend of witches,' they hissed at me when I left," Mama recounted. "Oh, I shall never forget it."

"Forget what? What's the commotion?" Father stood in the doorway of the company room. Only then did Mama lose her composure.

"Oh, Phillip." And she ran to him crying. "I am a friend of witches."

He held her in his arms while she blurted out her story again.

"You are the only true Christian amongst them," he pronounced. "Mary, I am prouder of you this day than I have ever been."

The next day a warrant was issued for the arrest of Sarah Cloyce. The afflicted girls had promptly gone into their fits again, first thing on Monday morning at Ingersoll's Ordinary, accusing Sarah of running out of Meeting on the Lord's Day. Certainly that made her a witch. None other than John Indian accused Sarah of tormenting him.

And while they were at the task, so as not to waste their time, I suppose, they cried out on John Proctor. For good measure they threw in little Dorcas Good, five-year-old daughter of Sarah. They said the little girl's shape had been running around biting them in retaliation for their crying out on her mother.

There was nothing I could do now, even if I had

a mind to. Anyone who spoke out against them was named or had someone in their family cried out on. The evil the girls had started had taken on a life of its own and was gaining momentum, like a ship under full sail with good trade winds behind it.

In the beginning of April, sisters Sarah Cloyce and Rebecca Nurse, Elizabeth Proctor and her husband, Martha Cory, and little Dorcas Good were taken across the marshes to Noddle's Island in a carriage and from there ferried to Boston, to prison.

At our house we settled in. April's cold rains slashed against the windows. Mama went no more to Meeting; nor did Mary. We gathered closer as a family. Thomas Hitchbourne continued to call on Mary. Mama worked in her shop, though trade fell off. Only faithful friends came in to purchase goods.

In our house we spoke no more of matters of witchcraft. What more could be said? Johnathan Hathorne called regularly and became one of us, sitting of an evening by the fire. He and his father were completely at odds, and that saddened him. Yet he held to his convictions.

He never spoke of the witchcraft proceedings or what he knew of them. And we never pressed him for information. But one evening, the second week of April, he began to talk quietly of the matter.

"Mary Warren has been arrested," he said. Everyone stared at him.

"She is one of the afflicted girls!" I cried.

"Yes, she is," Johnathan said. "But when her master, John Proctor, was arrested for a witch and sent to prison, she was left to care for his brood of children. Then the sheriff came and seized all the household goods in the Proctor house, as well as the cattle and foodstuffs. He even took the broth in the pot on the fire."

"How terrible!" Mama cried. "And what of the children?"

"Mary was left to care for them as best as she could. When matters worsened, she recanted her testimony and said she lied in court. So a warrant was issued for her. She is to appear before the magistrates and explain herself."

"One of the afflicted recanting her testimony against others? That is a good sign," Father said. "Perhaps there is hope."

Later that evening, I asked Johnathan to take me to see Mary Warren, who was being kept in an upstairs room at Ingersoll's Ordinary. He said yes. I had to see Mary. She must be strong enough to tell the truth, for the magistrates would believe her.

If I could not speak out myself, perhaps I could lend strength to Mary Warren to do so.

13

OUR LAST GOOD HOPE

"I DO THIS BE-cause I respect your father," Sarah Ingersoll told Johnathan as we followed her up the stairs in the ordinary. "But I'm weary of this whole witch nonsense. People say our business has improved for it. But all we do is feed and quench the hunger and thirst of the magistrates and marshals. And they don't pay their bills. We'll be billing for our services, ye can tell your father that. As well as for keeping the horses out back."

"My father appreciates everything you are doing," Johnathan told her.

We found Mary Warren seated in a chair in a corner of her room. No child; I knew her to be twenty if a day. But she looked like a frightened innocent, sitting there. She was a comely creature, her reddish hair escaping in tendrils from her white cap, which was clean and presentable, as were her apron and collar.

"I've made her proper for her examination later today," Sarah Ingersoll whispered. "I trust ye have come not to gawk at the poor child but to help."

"We are friends," Johnathan assured her.

She left us with Mary, who got up as we came into the room. "Why have you come here?" Clearly she was agitated, and she directed her question to Johnathan. "Your father is magistrate. Has he sent you? Even as the Devil sends his henchmen to wring the truth from me?"

"I do not come for my father," Johnathan said. "I come as a friend, with Susanna."

"I heard of your plight, Mary," I told her. "I have come to give you courage. And to beg you to tell them the truth about the circle."

"What do you know of it?"

But I was prepared for that question. "Nothing, I know nothing. I only suspect, as do many, that the girls are lying."

She laughed, a low, mocking sound. "I have told the magistrates this."

"Why did you not come forth sooner?" I asked.

"I was caught in a whirlwind. I come forth now to save my master. I am his jade."

This in itself was a confession, and I wondered if she would say such words in court. Did she indeed fancy herself in love with John Proctor? Had she had a sinful dalliance with him in his house? Was that why she had named his wife as a witch? To be rid of her? I had heard that Elizabeth Proctor was again with child.

"I love him," she said, answering my unspoken question. "Though my devotions have taken no sinful life of their own. I named his wife as a witch because Abigail Williams made me say that Elizabeth Proctor forced me to sign the Devil's book. 'Twas easy to do, as my mistress made me so miserable. But they promised me that if I named her, they would leave my master be."

So, the girls in the circle did not keep their promises, then.

"I begged my master not to speak out against them. You can't speak out against them or you are accused. Or someone in your family."

Was she warning me? Did she know of my conversation with Ann Putnam?

"They did break charity with me," she said softly. "So now I break charity with them."

I felt a surge of joy. So there was a rift in the circle now. As Father had said, this was a good sign. "You must be strong, Mary," I reminded her.

"Oh, I pray I can be! But when I try to tell the

magistrates the truth, I cannot speak. Something ties my tongue. My throat constricts. And the girls will be here, in Ingersoll's, today. For Abigail Hobbs, Bridget Bishop, and Giles Cory will be examined as witches."

"Abigail Hobbs?" I could not believe it.

"Oh yes. She's confessed to being a witch. And she's glad of it, too. Never have I seen one so glad. She came prancing up here this morning to see me. She was downstairs telling the patrons that she signed the Devil's book."

"Abigail Hobbs is no witch," I said. "She is . . ." But I stopped myself. 'Twas no business of mine if Abigail Hobbs wanted to be known as a witch. I would not pull her chestnuts out of the fire again. I had done so once and been made a fool of.

"I fear the other girls in the circle will make a mockery of me when I testify," Mary confided. She sat in the chair and broke into weeping.

I went to put my arm around her. She gripped my hand. "They are evil," she said. "They can make evil happen. And the magistrates choose to believe them over innocent people. I want to tell the truth, oh, I do! But they have sworn no one will break free of the circle, that if anyone tries she will suffer for it. I am so afraid."

Johnathan and I stayed with Mary in that room above the tavern. We quieted her and promised we would be in court. But in all honesty I did not think she would have the courage to go against the other girls in the circle.

Bridget Bishop came to testify that afternoon in Ingersoll's Ordinary, wearing her red paragon bodice. It was decorated with lace. Rain still pelted against the windows, cold and unrelenting, as if the heavens were shedding tears for what was about to transpire.

Abigail Hobbs was called to stand in front of the magistrates first. The crowd in the room hushed as she stood before Johnathan's father, Magistrate Corwin, and Reverends Parris and Noyes.

"I confess to the sin of witchcraft," Abigail Hobbs cried out in a firm voice that never wavered. "I am here to say that I have met with others in the coven in the Reverend Parris's pasture."

Everyone gasped. "I was at the last meeting of the coven," Abigail went on, warming to her subject. "I have seen the woman in the silk mantle, described by Tituba. I am here to say that I have committed murder!"

The magistrates asked her, quietly, whom she had killed.

"They were boys and girls. I do not know why I did such a thing. I was led to it by others in the coven."

"Who are these others?" Magistrate Hathorne asked.

"I know not their names. I know only that I have killed and seen blood flow. I have been a handmaiden of the Devil. I have sold my soul to ye Old Boy himself. I have summoned evil with sieves and keys, with nails and horseshoes."

To me, Abigail looked no different for such experiences. She was still tall and awkward in appearance, with long, disheveled hair falling about her shoulders, still without proper cap or shawl. She was dressed as if for a tramp in the woods. The magistrates whispered to one another.

"I have made a bargain with the Prince of Darkness so he can appear to others in my shape and hurt them," she added.

"Tell us how he does this," suggested Magistrate Corwin.

"It is not for me to give away the secret of his powers."

The judges became disgusted with her then and waved her away. As she was taken out by the marshals, she cried out to the magistrates, "I will be at your houses tonight. You will suffer torments!"

Bridget Bishop was brought in next.

"Mistress Bishop," said Magistrate Corwin, "you are accused of being a witch. How say you to this charge?"

"I do not know what a witch is."

Immediately the girls in the circle, who were sitting up front in the room, went into fits. They threw themselves on the floor and shrieked and wailed. They rolled their eyes.

"Do you not see their torment?" Corwin asked.

"They are in the silly season of their lives," Bridget answered calmly.

"You keep two ordinaries," Magistrate Hathorne reminded her. "You have been accused of allowing the young people to loiter in your ordinary at Salem Town until all hours of the night. You allow them to play shuffleboard. They make uproars when others sleep."

"This does not a witch make," she retorted.

The girls lay in a heap on the floor in front of her. They twitched their bodies and howled like forest creatures at the time of the full moon. The howling was a terrible thing to hear. It cut through one's bones with its primitive sound.

Magistrate Hathorne banged the table with his gavel. Mary Walcott screamed, "I see Bridget's shape up on that beam. Can't you see it? She sits there mocking me!"

At once, Mary Walcott's brother sprang out of the crowd of spectators, tore his sword from his side, and attacked the place where his sister pointed.

"He has ripped her cloak!" Mary cried out. "See? I heard it ripping!"

"I am innocent to a witch!" Bridget Bishop cried. "I know not what a witch is!"

"Take her away," boomed Magistrate Hathorne. And so she was taken.

Giles Cory was next. He was all of eighty, stoop shouldered, and white of hair. He shuffled down the aisle, as he was brought forward by two marshals.

"Untie his hands," Magistrate Hathorne said. The marshals did so. Immediately the afflicted girls gripped their own wrists and said they were being bitten.

"It is not enough to act the witch at other times?" Magistrate Hathorne asked Cory. "You must do it in the face of authority?"

"I am a poor creature and cannot help it," Cory whimpered.

"Bind his hands!" Magistrate Hathorne said. It was done. The girls stopped their howling. Giles Cory tilted his head, and all the girls tilted theirs in kind. He drew in his breath, pondering. They did likewise.

"Such a display of witchcraft is unheard of!" Magistrate Hathorne bellowed. "Take him away!"

The crowd hissed and booed as the old man was taken out. And then they brought in Mary Warren.

"I claim innocence to the charge of witchcraft, Your Honors," she said instantly.

Immediately John Indian and Gertrude Pope rolled to the floor and began tumbling about, clutching their stomachs.

This was too much for Mary Warren at the outset. "I look to God!" she cried out. "I look to God!"

Magistrate Corwin leaned across the table and gazed at her intently, but not without kindness in both voice and manner. "You were but a while ago an afflicted person. How comes this now to pass?"

"I will speak," Mary wailed. "Oh, I will speak."

"Do, girl, speak!" said Corwin.

Johnathan and I looked at each other and held our breaths. Would Mary now give evidence?

"She'll never do it," Johnathan whispered.

And she did not. She tried to speak but choked on her words as if the breath were being drawn out of her by invisible hands. She looked about to faint, but the marshals supported her on either side.

"Oh, I am sorry for it, I am sorry for it! O good Lord, help me! Save me!" she cried out.

"For what are you sorry?" Magistrate Hathorne asked.

"I will tell! I will tell! I will tell!" Mary screamed. But then she fell to the floor, seized by convulsions so bad that the marshals had to restrain her. And then, with everyone in the audience pressing forward to see her fit, and Magistrate Corwin ordering them back as general mayhem ensued, Magistrate Hathorne ordered that she be taken away. And so she was carried out, a lifeless form, to be placed in her upstairs room until she could sufficiently recover to speak again.

As she was being carried out, Ann Putnam, the younger, stood up and in a clear and childish voice explained what had happened to Mary Warren. "The shapes of Martha Cory and Elizabeth Proctor fell on her. They choked her. She fought them off."

"It is like seeing Christ fighting off the Devil in the wilderness," said Magistrate Hathorne. All agreed.

"Let's be gone from this place before I do or say something to have myself named," Johnathan said in disgust.

Outside, I welcomed the relief of rain, pure and cleansing. But there was a dreadful sadness in my soul. Mary Warren would never speak the truth, I could see that now. She would never break away from the circle. I felt a great draining of my spirit, a deep sense of hopelessness. "The truth will never be known now in Salem," I told Johnathan dismally.

But he was cheerful. "The truth will always come out somehow, Susanna," he told me. "Evil cannot prevail in such a place as this. We are good people. If there was one rift in the circle of girls, there can be another. Let's not lose hope."

As he helped me into his carriage, he spoke further on the matter. "I think we should not come to court again," he said. "No good comes from it. I myself will study my books and prepare for Harvard. You, Susanna, have better things to do, helping in your mother's shop. She needs your presence. Daily, I see the strain on her from worrying about William."

"You are right, Johnathan," I murmured.

"If those who remain sane amongst us make the same resolution, witchcraft in Salem will die out," he said. "I am convinced of it."

But witchcraft in Salem was not about to die out. For the girls in the circle had an insatiable appetite now for power and attention. They knew they could destroy anyone, that the magistrates hung on their every word. They would not stop. They had to keep going. It was expected of them.

The next day, nine more warrants were issued, more than ever before.

One was for my mother, Mary English.

14

THE SHIP IN THE SKY

⚜. THEY CAME AT night to arrest Mama. It was April 21. The rains of the past few weeks had stopped. The stars, in their fixed places in the heavens, shone brightly upon a Salem Town distilled with spring air.

But first something else happened:

In the hours before they came to arrest Mama I saw Tituba's ship of clouds in the sky.

I was hurrying up English Street so as not to be late for supper. I had been on a mission of mercy for Mama, to the house of George Jacobs. He was elderly and arthritic and lived alone. Mama had sent me with some supper in a pot. Jacob's maidservant, Sarah Churchill, was one of the afflicted girls and therefore too busy accusing people of witchcraft these days to cook for her master. And we conjectured that it would only be a short time before the sharp-tongued Jacobs, who was a town patriarch, would be cried out on. After all, hadn't he called the accusing girls "bitch witches"?

I was almost to our front gate when I saw the ship in the sky. A gust of wind blew off my cap, which went skipping down the street. I ran after it. As I picked it up, I stood drinking in the delicious wind that comes after rain. Overhead, the last of the clouds were being pushed out over the water. I could smell the sea and land fragrances, the lilac buds, and the scents of cherry and apple blossoms.

In the harbor, the sun—which had finally made an appearance this day—was setting. And against its redness the masts of three ships at anchor were etched darkly. I lingered, enjoying the scene. All up and down our street, beams of candlelight were thrown out of the windows onto the brick walks, and I felt a strange surge of peace working through me.

It was then that I saw the cloud in the shape of a ship.

It was above the horizon, as plain as if it were anchored in the harbor. It had a magnificent hull and stately masts, clearly outlined against the sky. It was fully rigged and majestic.

And just as Tituba had said, it flew the skull and crossbones.

I do not know how much time transpired as I stood there, my eyes fixed on that apparition. I was aware of footsteps on the street, of people passing as I dallied, but no one else took notice of my ship in the sky. I heard the night watch calling the hour, six bells; the cries of the gulls swooping overhead; the bark of a dog somewhere; the clop, clop, clopping of a horse pulling a carriage. All these distinct sounds anchored me to the real world.

But my eyes never moved from that vision. Then, just as Tituba had predicted, the shape of the flag seemed to melt from that of a skull and crossbones into that of an English banner, the kind my father flew on his ships. After a few minutes, the outline of the ship changed into a plain cloud again. And I heard Tituba's words: *When this happens, your William will soon be back.*

Oh, William, I thought, to think you will be coming home! A rush of happiness flooded me and I hurried to our door, anxious to tell my family. Then I remembered Tituba's admonition to tell no one. And I recollected how my friendship with her was still a secret.

Her other words came to me, also: *The air is black over Salem. The sun is gone from this place.*

As I sat at our table, Tituba's dour words receded in my mind. I felt only happiness while in the bosom of my family. Father was full of news from Boston, having just visited his shipyard there. Mary was happily awaiting Thomas Hitchbourne. She had confided to me earlier that he was going to ask our father for her hand this evening.

Apparently she had already told Mama, also, for there were special cakes set out in the company room with the claret for Thomas's arrival. And when he came, he went immediately to the library with Father. Mary was jumping out of her skin, she was so anxious, although she tried to sit properly and work at her crewel by the fire. Mama's face beamed with happiness and pride, and in general there was a great feeling of benevolence all around.

When Thomas and Father emerged from the library, Father's face was wreathed in smiles. "Mary, we have a new member of the family," he said. "Or soon will have."

There were a few moments in which everyone hugged everyone else. There were plans, toasting, laughter. Thomas blushed and told us the marriage would be a year hence, but Mary and Mama were already plotting the festivities. And I glowed secretly inside for the knowledge that William would probably be home for the wedding.

We had the most pleasant evening I could recollect in a long time. And then everything cruelly changed.

Mama had retired to her bedchamber, Father to his library. I was in my bedroom reading when the marshals came. There was a dreadful pounding on the door, and those servants who went to respond to it tried to resist the men who stood there.

Father came out of his library, Mary and Thomas out of the company room, I down from my bedroom. The light from the marshals' lantern spilled into our hallway. Father bade them enter and to read their warrant.

Mama sent down word that she would not resist arrest, but neither would she come down this night. Mary burst into tears and Thomas looked grim. I paled. My hands were like ice, and I was shaking. The marshals went up the stairway with Father and read Mama the warrant while she sat up in bed listening.

Then she sent them from the room, called for Mary and me, and hugged and kissed us, then bade us go to bed. "I am prepared," she said. "I have been expecting this since the day I sat with Sarah Cloyce in Meeting. Don't cry, Susanna. You must be strong now. This is a misunderstanding. We will clear up the matter. The magistrates are not demented. Go now, both of you; I must talk with your father."

I did not sleep that night. I tossed and turned in torment and guilt. I could not understand this. Ann Putnam had promised they would not touch anyone in my family. What had happened?

Oh, I was so angry! I would go in the morning, I decided, and tell the magistrates what I knew!

No, tomorrow I would go to Ann Putnam herself. I would confront her and make the girls take back their charge against my mother. I must!

I could barely wait for morning. I got out of bed to see a full moon and shreds of clouds still moving against a clear sky. I remembered my ship. Had that peace becalmed me only a few hours earlier? Tonight my family had been so happy together. Had the fates given us this one last night together, then, before we were to be destroyed?

Oh, I must stop thinking such! Looking out the windows, I could see the shapes of the guards walking around our house. I ran back to bed and hid under the covers. Toward morning I fell asleep. Mary woke me and bade me come down and have breakfast with the family.

Mama was at peace. It was as if the fearful event that had been weighing down on her for weeks had finally happened and nothing could hurt her anymore. She sat with us at breakfast as if nothing was amiss, giving instructions to Mary and me as to the running of the household and the shop, as if she was going on a pleasure trip to Boston.

She called in the servants and gave them instructions. "The herbs must be planted in the kitchen garden," she instructed them. "Farming in all of Salem has been sadly neglected this spring because of this witch business. Deborah, you are in charge of the house servants, and you will report to Mary or Susanna. They know what must be done."

We had morning devotions, and then she went with the marshals. Father promptly got into his own carriage and left to see what could be done about Mama's arrest. The house was cold and empty. I ached with the loneliness of it. How could this have happened? Mama gone? She had always been here. *How could they take my mother?*

I put on my cloak. "Where are you off to?" Mary asked.

"To see Johnathan," I lied. "Mayhap he can talk to his father."

Once again it was Mercy Lewis who let me in the Putnam house. I could not help noticing some change in her. Always a tall girl but previously rather stoop-shouldered, she now stood erect and proud. Her voice was stronger, her movements sure.

"You are a friend of Abigail Hobbs, are you not?" she asked.

"I knew her in dame school," I said.

"She has brought her condition on herself. She always disparaged community decency." And it was as if, in that dim and candle-lit hallway, Abigail Hobbs was already condemned. I yearned to tell this arrogant girl the real reason for Abigail's past behavior. But I bit back my words. Everything one said to them, they used against one.

"She's no more a witch than I am," I said.

"We have named her."

"Does that make her a servant of the Devil?"

"We are believed." She smiled at me. "Abigail has named her parents as witches. This day they were taken with your mother and Edward Bishop, stepson of Bridget; his wife, Sarah; Mary Esty; Sarah Cloyce; and Sarah Wilds."

"You have been busy, I see."

"They are confessing."

"To save their lives. But my mother will never confess! You won't get away with this!"

"Get away with what?" Young Ann Putnam appeared in the hall. One minute she was not there and the next she was, rooted in the flickering shadows.

I was trembling with loathing. "You promised me that if I kept my mouth sealed, you would not cry out on my family!"

She smiled and tilted her head. Her eyes glittered. "I have not broken charity with you."

"You named my mother a witch!"

"Yes." And she sighed sadly. "It was something that had to be done."

I had never known such rage. I felt it boiling in my veins, one with my blood. How dare this pale, sickly slip of a girl, this half woman who was so enmeshed in evil, assume the power of defaming the innocent? I stood there clenching and unclenching my fists. I wanted to jump on her, to seize her and choke the life out of her, and if they named me a witch, so be it.

Ann Putnam stepped forward. "Your mother sealed her fate the day she sat with Sarah Cloyce in church. Your silence could no longer protect her."

"Do you know so little of love and charity that you cannot distinguish it from evil?"

"We do the Lord's work," she answered simply. "An army of devils is horribly broke in upon this place. And the houses of the good people are filled with the doleful shrieks of their children and servants. The Devil is about to make his last struggle for dominion in our world, fulfilling the prophecies of David and the mystery of the Apocalypse."

"You are mad," I said. "Pure and simple. You are demented." I looked from her to Mercy. "All of you are mad."

"We must expose Satan's servants," Ann Putnam went on as if I hadn't spoken. "Witches abound in

Salem and Topsfield, and if those named deliver other names to us, they will serve their purpose and be forgiven."

"My mother needs no one's forgiveness," I lashed out at her. "Least of all yours."

"She has put away God's ordinances. She has befriended a witch. It was our duty to name her."

I stared at the two of them. And then a thought came to me like the wind across the sky, pushing the dark clouds of anger out of the way. "You believe what you are doing," I said in cold wonder. And I felt the uselessness of argument. For if this was true, if the girls in the circle had indeed started believing their own lies, then all was lost.

"Of course," she answered. "Why should we not? Do you think we take this charge from the Lord lightly?"

"It started as sport," I reminded her. "The last time we spoke, you said you had accepted the diagnosis of the evil hand on you to get attention."

"We were not sensible yet of what was happening with us. We thought it sport. But when we name people, they confess to horrible doings we do not even accuse them of. And when an accused witch confesses, a great peace comes over us."

I looked from Ann to Mercy. "You have become enamored with your own lies," I said.

They both shrugged.

"You are drunk with your own powers. But what of Mary Warren, who still languishes in prison? She knows right from wrong. What if she tells that you all dissemble?"

"She will not tell," Ann Putnam said. "She is not strong enough. She knows the only way to save herself now is to come back into our circle. She will reaffirm everything we say, or we will destroy her."

I drew in my breath sharply. It felt like a knife in my chest. "Is there no heart left in you to appeal to, Ann?"

I meant it. If there was the smallest chance that I could humble myself before her, I would do it. I would do it for Mama. Though I loathed this girl thoroughly.

"My heart is pure," she insisted. "I rest assured that we are giving our ministers and magistrates and elders what they crave."

I turned to go. Mercy handed me my cloak. "You will not get my mother in your evil web," I told Ann. "I don't know what I will do, but I will do something."

She saw me to the door and smiled sweetly. "Do not attempt to tell lies about us, Susanna English, or the rest of your family will be named. You have a sister, remember. And a father. And a brother, due back any day now from a sea voyage, am I correct?"

I stood on the stone threshold outside the door as

a gust of wind came around the corner of the house. I looked to the sky. A huge black cloud covered the sun. When I had entered the house, the sky had been a clear blue.

Her smile sickened me. "Your mother went willingly with the marshals this morning. She was saying something about paying gladly for her sins and would accept this penance rather than lose your brother. Your mother has made her peace with the Lord. I would not interfere, were I you. Or others in your family will be named."

I knew I could not speak out now. For these girls did, indeed, have some dark powers. And they could hurt the rest of my family. I turned and fled, got into my cart, and rode away without looking back.

15

THE CAT AND THE WHEEL

AS MOLASSES bounded through the familiar lanes of Salem Village, the sights of budding trees and pussy willows and colorful flowers pushing their heads up through meadow grasses flashed by. Spring had come, but in my heart it was still winter.

I saw these signs of new life all around me as blasphemy. How could nature honor us with such hope when ugliness and the rotting nature of evil had their grip on this place?

"Susanna! Susanna English!" I heard my name called but did not pull in the reins.

"Susanna, is the Devil himself chasing you?"

And then Johnathan Hathorne was beside me, running to keep pace with my cart. I pulled up on the reins, and once Molasses stopped, I became sensible of the fact that tears were coming down my face, that my hat and cloak were askew, my hair loose and ragged.

"Susanna, what ails you? You were going at a breakneck speed. If your horse had tripped, you could have been killed."

His familiar and dear voice cut through my restraint, and I felt the hot tears flow.

"Susanna. I know. I heard what happened. Dear Susanna, these are dark circumstances, indeed. I went to your house, and Mary told me you had gone out to seek me. I've been looking for you, to comfort you."

He touched my shoulder, and my remaining restraint fled. In the next instant, I was leaning out of the cart and he was holding me in his arms.

"Susanna, I curse the fates that cause my father to be part of this! When I heard that he had issued the warrant for your mother's arrest, I stormed out of the house, but not before we had the worst of confrontations. All the servants were cowering in corners. It wouldn't surprise me if the door were barred against me this night."

He lifted me out of the cart and held me close for a moment, quieting my tears. "Don't despair. I hear your father is pursuing every means to help your mother. His carriage drew up at our door right after I left."

"Do you think your father gave him any hope?"

"I don't know what transpired between them. But Phillip English is not without power and influence, you know."

"The afflicted girls are the ones with all the power, Johnathan. Whatever they say, they are believed."

"Don't lose hope. There is still much hidden. It will come out in the trials."

"Do you think so, Johnathan?"

"I am sure of it. As sure as I am of another matter."

"What is that?"

"That you have, in me, a friend, Susanna. That I can't bear to witness your tears. That I will come at any hour of the day or night, with my sword if necessary. You have only to send a servant for me."

His strong hands held mine, warm and reassuring. He was so innocent, I minded, to think he could strike with his sword the malignancy that had come to live amongst us. But his words did warm me and lift the anguish from my heart.

At home a fire burned cheerily in the company room, for the day had turned overcast. Deborah was setting bread and cheese and meat and wine out on our dining board, and she summoned Mary and me for a noon repast.

As we waited at the table for Father, I felt a renewed flush of despair when my eye fell on Mama's empty chair. But then the front door burst open and Father came in. "Daughters, there is good news! I have a letter from William!"

William? Joy replaced my pain. The room seemed to brighten. "And there is more news," Father said, taking his place at the head of the table and pouring some wine. "I went to Magistrate Hathorne this morning. I gained a special indulgence for your mother. She will not be sent to Salem Prison. She is at the Cat and the Wheel. She has her own room there, and we may go and see her tomorrow before she is examined."

"Oh, the Cat and the Wheel is a commodious tavern," Mary said. "Surely this is a good sign. Can't we go this afternoon?"

"Nay, I go alone this afternoon. We have much to speak of."

"Then you must bring her some fresh bread and cheese and broth," Mary suggested.

As he read us William's letter, between sips of claret, the room seemed to fill with a lightness, as if the sun had come out. Every object stood out with a clarity of form heretofore unknown to me. And hearing William's words, which had come to us from far across the sea, I pondered: There *are* forces in the world that we cannot see, and they are for good as well as for evil. And I sensed, with an inner certainty, that the forces of good were far more powerful than the forces of evil.

However, William was writing from prison in Guadeloupe, where he had languished now for these past six months awaiting trial as a pirate.

"A day's sailing from Barbados," Father read, "when we were heading for Martinique, a suspicious ship appeared on the horizon and gave chase. As the distance between us closed, I saw she flew a skull and crossbones from her forepeak. I ordered all hands to ready the cannon. We fired at the pirate vessel and our six pounders did her much damage, but she continued on toward us.

"She came closer and closer, as if borne by some winds we had no benefit of. It was an eerie experience. Finally, this parcel of mongrel thieves overtook the *William and Susanna*, boarded us by throwing grapnels across to our ship, and made their way across our decks. My crew fought bravely. In the brawl that followed, the pirates lost more men than we. But too many of us were wounded. And these pirates, who use their vengeful power without the least respect for humanity, forced us to join their ranks, since their crew was diminished.

"They took us aboard. I am sorry to say, Father, that they scuttled the *William and Susanna* after taking all the goods in her hold. I was wounded and allowed to recover, but once improved I was forced, with the rest of my men, to take part in sailing their galleon. We were part of their hellish crew for at least six weeks. Then, one night, when the waters were becalmed and we were off the coast of French-owned Guadeloupe, my men were in charge while theirs were sleeping. We headed the ship into a light wind, lashed the wheel, and dropped a small boat over the side with provisions and firearms. Then we rowed for shore.

"But once on land, because of our garb—which we were forced to wear by our captors—we were arrested as pirates. For months we awaited trial in prison. It came two weeks ago, but we had no proof of our identities, since everything had been taken from us. And since many French, English, and Dutch men take to the sea as desperados, the judges thought us such. So, back to prison we went.

"Our trial, however, was not unfruitful. For the captain of a ship from Massachusetts Bay Colony was in court, seeking pirates who had plundered many of his vessels. He recognized my name. And since our name is much respected amongst seamen and merchants, it turned out that the pirates had not taken everything from me. This captain's ship is due to sail, but he will be taking the time to come to prison to see me. I will give him this letter for you. He gave a good accounting of me to the magistrates here, who have promised to release us when the next ship for the colonies puts into port.

"We must stay in prison because French authorities want us in safety, since feeling against those even suspected of piracy is very bad hereabouts. But I have their promise that our lot will improve. Already, I have been given writing materials, and we have been well fed. And one of the magistrates has invited me to his home for dinner. He is French, and they say he has a beautiful daughter. The captain of the ship from Massachusetts Bay Colony brought me clothes befitting my station in life. They say another ship is due in June—three months away. Pray we will be on it. I send most affectionate greetings to Mother and the girls and live in anticipation of seeing you soon. I remain your devoted son, William."

At first light the next morning, Mary came to my room. The fires in the hearth were still low from the night. We took breakfast in the kitchen with the servants, then, bundled against the morning chill, took the horse and carriage to the Cat and the Wheel to see Mama. Father had left early for Boston.

In hand we had a pot of warm broth and some fresh corn bread and cheese. Father had brought her the letter from William yesterday afternoon.

We found Mama at prayers, dressed and smiling in her small room upstairs. She hugged us, hushed our wails, accepted our offerings, and smilingly bade us kneel on the floor beside her to give thanks to the Almighty for delivering William back to us alive. She was happier than I remembered seeing her in months.

As we sat at the small table in her room, she bade us speak softly, then, doing so herself, recited breathlessly that the examining judges were staying in the room next door.

"Only the thinnest of walls divides us," she whispered. "Last night I set my chair next to this wall and overheard their conversations. I took notes on what they said."

"What did they say, Mama?" I asked.

"They have the written complaint of Susannah Sheldon against Bridget Bishop. It also condemns me."

I gasped. "How can such be?"

She put her hand over mine on the table and smiled. The sweetness of her smile smote my heart. "They were reading the complaint last night. They read that on the fourth day of April, at night, came Goody Bishop, Goody English, Goodman Giles Cory, and a tall man with a high-crowned hat. They read that we had books in our hands, and that Goody Bishop bade them touch her book. Susannah Sheldon testified she would not do it. And then there came a stretched snake creeping over Goody Bishop and into her bosom. Susannah Sheldon claimed that I had a yellow bird in my bosom, and Goodman Cory had two turtles hanging onto his coat. And that he opened his coat and put the turtles to his breast and gave them suck."

"Oh!" Mary started to go white in the face.

"I know now of what they will accuse me," Mama said with satisfaction. "And I will tell them that on the fourth day of April, at night, I was home with my family."

"Susannah Sheldon speaks of your spectral shape, Mama," I reminded her. "Of the Devil assuming your shape and flying about and hurting others."

"I know that. But many people of high esteem in the community do not believe in spectral evidence. I shall question the judges about that. I shall warn them that the superior courts will review their decisions. I shall not be afraid. For I learned something else, listening at the wall last night."

"What did you learn, Mama?" we asked in unison.

"They had a heated argument. As high sheriff, George Corwin has been made to confiscate the property, livestock, and personal possessions of everyone accused of witchcraft. Magistrate Jonathan Corwin argues that the property should not be confiscated until the person goes to trial and is accused. Magistrate Hathorne thinks the property should be immediately confiscated."

Mary and I looked at each other. "It's what they did to John Proctor's household," I said.

"The point is, the two magistrates are arguing," Mama said, "as they argued over Mary Warren. Corwin says they must be kinder when questioning her in the future. Hathorne would give her no quarter."

"Mama, I still fear for you," I said.

"Don't. These magistrates are not as sure of themselves as they appear. Nor are the ministers. They struggle with legal matters and theology. God is with us. Didn't He let us know that William is still alive? Now we have other matters to discuss, so listen."

And she proceeded to advise us. Neither Mary nor I must appear at her examination this day. "If the girls see you, they may cry out on you. Those who are not before their sights, they are less likely to name. Did your father leave for Boston this morning?"

"Early," I told her.

"He is trying to make arrangements for me to be removed there. If, by any happenstance, your father is named as a witch, and I have every reason to suspect he will be, he has plans to flee. We discussed it and prayed on it. At first word of a warrant being issued, he will set about eluding the authorities. At this juncture, I want you both to go and stay with Joseph and Elizabeth Putnam. We have made arrangements for that, too. Our servants will take care of the house. Your father has enough influence to keep our property from being confiscated until he goes to trial."

Mary and I stared at each other.

She went on. "The Putnams are good people."

Mary was sobbing. "I don't want us to be apart," she said.

"We won't be for long, Mary," Mama said. "Your father will be caught, eventually. But by then he hopes to have everything in order so we will both be in Boston. And we want you girls to come with us."

"To jail?" Mary asked.

"No, Mary," Mama said soothingly. "Father is using his influence so we can have our liberty in Boston and only report to jail at night. We would have you girls stay with friends there."

Immediately I felt panic. "What of William?" I asked. "Someone should be here to give William fair warning when he steps off the ship. The afflicted girls know of him. They may cry out on him. And someone should be here to tell him where his family has gone."

"The Putnams can do that for us," Mama said.

"He may put in at the harbor before they know he is back," I argued. I had a reason for arguing. I cared about William, yes, but the real demon in my breast was guilt.

I wanted to stay in Salem when Mama and Father

and Mary went to Boston. Here was some way I could make up for not speaking out about the circle in the beginning.

I was the cause of this mayhem and fury in Salem, after all. As much as the demented girls. For they now believed their own lies. I knew them to be untruths. And I might still get the opportunity to speak out if I stayed.

If there was the smallest possibility that such an opportunity should be awarded to me, I could not run away.

"Mama, let me stay with the Putnams, even if you all go to Boston," I begged. "You, yourself, said they are good people. And Johnathan Hathorne has pledged his friendship to me. He said he would come to my aid with his sword if trouble came. You know he is on our side."

She nodded. "I know he is smitten with you, Susanna. And you with him."

I blushed. "I do love him, Mama. Please don't blame him for what his father does."

"Neither your father nor I blame Johnathan for what his father does," she said. "We both see Johnathan has grown well into manhood and knows his own mind. But you two profess love for one another. He'll visit you at the Putnams, if you stay, as he visited you at our home. This places undue burden on the Putnams, Susanna."

"Please, Mama," I begged. "Johnathan is honorable. And I wouldn't do anything to dishonor you and Father. Please let me stay."

We all looked at each other. Mama sighed. "We will pray on it," she said.

And so we prayed. I don't know what Mary prayed for. She hadn't protested going to Boston. But she and Thomas Hitchbourne were betrothed. And Thomas did not have a stern magistrate for a father, who would forbid him to visit Mary in Boston.

After a few moments, Mama raised her head. "One of the things you will someday learn, daughter," she said to me, "is that parents are never sure if certain decisions we make concerning our children are right."

I held my breath and waited.

"We can ponder them, pray on them. I have anguished often over many decisions your father and I made about our children. But thus far you have all done us proud. So I will go with my instincts and the Lord's help."

She sighed. "You may stay with the Putnams if we all go to Boston. But you must promise me: If at any given moment, Joseph Putnam determines it is time to take his own family and flee, you will go with them, William or no William. Johnathan or no Johnathan."

"Thank you, Mama. I promise."

"And you must always behave, at the Putnams', in

a proper manner, which will never bring dishonor on your family."

I promised that, too.

We stayed awhile longer with her. Mama was examined that afternoon and sent to Salem Prison. Mary and I packed our possessions at home, to be in readiness to go to the Putnams if a warrant was issued for Father.

We went once that week to see Mama in Salem Prison. It was such a terrible place that Mary and I wept openly. But Mama was so busy attending to the other women that she could not abide our tears. And she bade us go home and wait for Father's return from Boston.

A week after Father returned, in the hour before dawn when the sky was bathed in an eerie yellow light, there came a pounding on our front door.

It was Johnathan Hathorne, come to warn us that this day his father would write a warrant for the arrest of Phillip English.

Father fled immediately. Mary and I went to the Putnams.

16

ANOTHER CIRCLE IN SALEM

🌿 "YOU'D BEST put another plate on the board, Susanna. I see my husband has brought company for supper again."

Elizabeth Putnam held five-month-old Mary on her shoulder as she turned from the hearth to peer out the kitchen window toward the barnyard. It was a fine day in late May. Beyond the open kitchen door all the world beckoned, alive with the scents and sounds of an afternoon in late spring. The mellow light of sunset bathed the door frame.

"Now whom has he brought this time?" Elizabeth asked. But I picked up the note of bemused fondness in her voice. For in the month that Mary and I had been living with the Putnams we had learned that

Elizabeth and Joseph loved each other very much. And their caring devotion extended to all those they welcomed into their home.

Elizabeth patted baby Mary as we watched Joseph and another man, deep in conversation, walk their horses slowly toward the barn. Then she smiled at me. "It's Johnathan Hathorne. You'd best go change that collar. The baby has spit up on you."

I ran upstairs to do her bidding. My heart was beating very fast, as it did every time I saw Johnathan, although he had come to call often in the time I'd been here. As had Thomas Hitchbourne. The Putnams had welcomed both young men and given Mary and I our privacy with our suitors.

The room Mary and I shared was on the second floor, across from Joseph and Elizabeth's. Indeed, they had done their utmost to make us feel like kin. I had many bitter moments when I mourned Mama, who was still in Salem Prison; and though we didn't know where Father was, though matters in our community were moving swiftly toward even greater turmoil, in this sturdy three-story house, we felt protected.

We were assigned no real duties. But I quickly took stock when we arrived and determined that since the house was large and they had only two indentured servants, the house girl and her husband, and there was a new baby to care for, Elizabeth could use our help. So I set about assisting her with the child and Mary helped with the sewing and cooking.

I was most pleased, of course, to discover that my original impressions of Joseph Putnam had been correct. He was not only a mixture of sober strength and boyish eagerness, but he was gentle with his wife and baby, caring of his neighbors, and quick to enjoy a good joke. He behaved toward us in the manner of an older brother. Elizabeth, meanwhile, took the role of older sister, glad to have two females about who were not servants and in whom she could confide her secret joys and fears.

Mama had been right in wanting us here, I decided. I changed my collar and brushed my hair. In the time I had been here, I had discovered something else that warmed my heart.

Joseph Putnam was emerging as the leader of a new circle in Salem.

The circle, as I perceived it, was composed of people who knocked on his door in the middle of the night, who sat with Joseph by candlelight in his library, talking until dawn, when they appeared at the board for breakfast. Others rode to his place to talk with him in the barn, while their wives came and sat, midday, to speak with Elizabeth.

These were people like Reverend Johnathan Hale from Beverly and the kinsmen of Rebecca Nurse. And Thomas Maule, a Quaker who held with the belief that the witchcraft business had started from petty hatreds in the neighborhood. Some were people who had once come to Mama's shop—like Reverend Wise of Ipswich, who had spoken in behalf of John Proctor, and Reverend Francis Dane of Andover, who was trying to caution his flock about the witch panic.

And there were others who corresponded from Boston. One name I had come to know was Thomas Brattle, a merchant and learned mathematician, who was about to be named treasurer of Harvard College. Another was Robert Calef, a merchant friend of Brattle's, who was equally outspoken against witchcraft.

I sensed, though Joseph had not actually told me, that these people were all working quietly in the background, waiting for the right moment to step forward and take a stand.

Every Monday morning Joseph took us to visit Mama in Salem Prison. We were allowed only one visit a week by the authorities, but Mary and I made the best of it. Mary cooked delicacies to bring; I took bundles of clean clothing. We knew Mama shared the food, but we did not chide her. In prison with her were Sarah Morey, Lydia Dustin, Susannah Martin, and Dorcas Hoar, along with Margaret Jacobs and Mary Esty.

While we visited with Mama, Joseph visited with

the male prisoners. When we took our leave he paid the jailer two shillings and sixpence, which was Mama's board for the week.

Father had left money with him for this purpose and any other concerning our family. If Joseph knew where Father was, he did not divulge this fact to us. And Mary and I agreed we would not badger him to tell us.

And so the weeks of May went by. Many times, sensing that Joseph and Elizabeth were working as leaders of this new circle, I had considered coming forth and telling them what I knew.

Then I thought of Mary Warren, who had tried to recant her testimony. I pondered how the magistrates had badgered her. Finally she broke. Denying that her original testimony had been false, she started talking about shapes hovering over her again. The magistrates were happy. They announced that she was cleansed of her sin, and she rejoined the circle.

So, then, who would believe me? Joseph and Elizabeth, yes. But Father was still in danger. The magistrates had widened their search for him to include Boston. And there was Mary to think about. I did not care for myself, but I could not risk the girls crying out on Mary. Let alone brother William when he returned. So I kept my silence. The time for speaking out would come, I told myself. And when it did come, I would know it.

We were at the Putnams' only two days when I learned something else about them:

One morning I'd gone to the henhouse to collect eggs so Mary could make breakfast. As I passed the barn, I looked in the open door and saw the horses fully saddled in their stalls.

"Jed must have forgotten to unsaddle the horses," I said to Ellen, their maidservant, as I handed the eggs to Mary and took my seat at the table.

From across the table, Joseph frowned and sipped his morning brew. When Ellen left the room, he looked at me and Mary. "Girls, I must tell you this. But you must keep it quiet. Can you?"

We both assented. "Have I done something to displease you, sir?" I asked. He looked so solemn.

He smiled. "You must call me Joseph, both of you. We must be friends, with no secrets between us. We must trust one another in this house. For our safety depends one upon the other."

We must have no secrets. Those words were like a knell in my bones. "Yes, Joseph," I said.

"I keep my horses saddled at all times. And we have bags packed. It would please me if you would both pack bags and leave them by your bedsides. Elizabeth is able to use a firearm. Are either of you?"

I stared at placid, sweet Elizabeth. She smiled back. "No," I said numbly. Mary shook her head and stared at him, wide-eyed.

"I shall teach you both."

"Has it come to this, then?" I asked.

"Mayhap it will. Being related to my brother serves me no longer. I have alienated us from the authorities by the stand I took. If we are accused, we intend to flee in the night. And you will both come with us."

"Yes, Joseph," I said.

I tied a ribbon in my hair. Blue. It had come from Mama's shop. I went back downstairs. In the kitchen, Johnathan was seated at the table with Joseph and Elizabeth.

"Hello, Susanna," he said.

He and Joseph had been deep in conversation. No doubt, Johnathan appreciated the older cousin he had in Joseph. For though he still lived under his father's roof, the elder Hathorne had all but disowned him. And it pained Johnathan greatly.

We listened as the two men told of how Mary Esty, who had been released from prison earlier this month for lack of evidence, was again arrested. Mercy Lewis had taken ill and said that she saw Mary's shape hovering over her.

"Of course," Joseph said dryly, "my niece and Abigail Williams were at Mercy's bedside, seeing the shape, also."

Elizabeth lighted candles on the table. They cast

long, flickering shadows, and I grew dismal. We ate, for a moment, in silence. Then Joseph laughed.

"They brought John Alden into court this afternoon, Elizabeth."

John Alden, firstborn of John and Priscilla of Plymouth Colony, was a well-known sea captain, soldier, and Indian fighter. And a friend of Joseph's.

"He strode into the courtroom," Joseph recounted, "and when the girls fell into fits, he said they were doing juggling tricks. He called them Salem wenches. Bartholomew Gedney was sitting on the bench with the other magistrates. He almost laughed when the girls accused Alden of selling powder and shot to the Indians and of having Indian papooses. Gedney said that if such practices make a man a witch, half the men of Massachusetts Bay Colony could be so accused."

He laughed again, but Elizabeth was solemn. "What happened to John Alden?" she asked.

Joseph sobered. "I don't think for one God-given moment that Gedney believed the charges. But the others did, and he gave in to them. Alden was taken away, calling the girls liars. He's posted bail and is in his own home under guard."

"He is a brave man," said Elizabeth. "But bravery does naught in that court."

"We'll stand behind him, Elizabeth, dear. But now I have other news. Last week the frigate *Nonesuch* put in at Boston Harbor. Increase Mather has returned with our new charter. And with our new royal governor, Sir William Phips."

Everyone asked about the charter and what Joseph had heard of it.

"We will still be allowed to elect our own representatives to the General Court of Massachusetts Bay Colony," he told us. "And all our land titles have been reinstated. But hear this! The electorate is not limited to members of the covenant—those Puritans who consider their salvation secure. Anyone, from any Christian sect, may be elected. Can you believe this? Susanna and Mary, your father will be pleased."

"He always wanted something like this," I agreed.

Joseph laughed and slapped his knee. "The damned can rule! Oh, I tell you, Mather and Phips will have their troubles now. The Puritans will have difficulty accepting this."

"Tell me of this Phips," Elizabeth insisted. "Is he the same who was born on that rude plantation on the River Kennebec in Maine?"

"The same," Joseph said. "His father was a gunsmith; his mother gave birth to twenty-six children. He's the one who built a ship when he was twenty-one and sailed off to the Bahamas to retrieve that sunken treasure from a Spanish galleon, bushels and bushels of pieces of eight."

He turned to Mary and me, explaining, "He took

it to England and was knighted. He could have lived there in high style, but he's a New Englander at heart. Always he pushed the king for restoration of our rights. He was named the new royal governor when he helped Mather secure our new charter at the court of King William."

"Which side will he take about witchcraft?" Elizabeth mused.

"Elizabeth, my dear, when a man grows up in the wilds of Maine, where the wind crackles in the trees at night and the wolves are thicker than they are here, where the deaths of infants and livestock are wrought as if by unseen hands, he believes in witches," Joseph told her.

"Oh," Elizabeth said sadly.

"Yes." Joseph refilled his mug. "Maine does something to a man's soul. So when Sir William Phips was told that witches have broken out all over the place, he believed the story."

"And besides," Johnathan added, "he has sailed the Spanish Main. And heard all the fanciful tales of the Devil and sea monsters."

"You two certainly are cheerful this evening," Elizabeth remarked.

"My dear, we tell the truth. Phips will do his duty. They say he is setting up a court to try the accused. It will be called the Court of Oyer and Terminer. They sit on June the second."

"From whence the name?" Elizabeth asked.

"It means 'to hear and determine,' " Joseph explained.

"And who," Elizabeth persisted, "will hear and determine about our accused friends and neighbors?"

"Bartholomew Gedney from Salem. Sam Sewall, John Richards, William Sargeant, and Wait Winthrop from Boston. Nathaniel Saltonstall from Haverhill. The presiding justice will be Deputy Governor Stroughton."

"And Governor Phips?" Elizabeth asked.

"Sir William has assigned himself a safer mission," Joseph reported. "He has gone off to fight Indians."

Joseph summoned me and Mary into his library after supper. "First, you and Johnathan may have the company room again this evening, as I have given it to Mary and Thomas," he said to me. "With the same consideration—that Johnathan leaves at ten o'clock."

I waited. He had not summoned us here to tell us such. Then he went on. "I have had word today of a disturbing matter regarding the prisoners in Salem Prison."

My mouth went dry. I heard Mary utter a suppressed sob. Had something happened to Mother? But Joseph held up his hand and shook his head, allaying our fears.

"Your mother is well. But they have put chains on the prisoners. When Sir William heard that the shapes of the accused witches are still flying about the countryside afflicting the girls, he ordered chains."

Mary threw her arms around me and began to weep. I held her and stood strong. *Mama in chains!* How could I bear it?

Joseph came to us and put one hand on Mary's head and the other on my shoulder. "There now, girls, the news is not all bad. When your father heard of this in Boston, he made ready to come back to Salem and turn himself in. He has been working all this time to have your mother removed to Boston. He returns in hopes of making things easier for her. He is prepared to face charges."

Mary's crying intensified. "What will happen to him when he returns?" she wailed.

"He will be examined. But because of his position, he and your mother will be allowed their liberties in Boston, returning to Arnold's Jail only at night."

"You've been helping him, haven't you, Joseph?" I said. "We are much beholden to you."

"I am working for many others, also." He smiled. "You girls must have become sensible of that. I wanted to prepare you both, this evening, for the fact that your father may be knocking at our door any night now. I wanted you to be ready to receive him.

Mary, you're to go with your parents to Boston, I understand. Is that so?"

Mary wiped her eyes. "Yes, sir."

"Susanna, as I understand it, your mother said you may stay with us. We are happy to have you. But are you sure this is what you want to do, child?"

"Yes, sir. If you'll have me."

He nodded solemnly. "We're glad to have you. Now go and help your sister pack her things."

17

WHEN I HEAR THE OWLS CALL AT NIGHT

🌿 FATHER CAME knocking on the Putnam door that very night. More correctly, it was near three in the morning on the thirtieth of May. I thought I was dreaming when the sound of thumping awoke me. I jumped out of bed and saw, in the light of the full May moon that flooded the yard, a figure on horseback. I heard Joseph in the hall, then going down the stairs. I woke Mary and went out into the hall, where Elizabeth stood in her nightdress, holding a candle.

She put a finger to her lips and shushed us. Only then did it occur to me that the figure outside on horseback might be a marshal come to arrest the Putnams.

The eerie light from Elizabeth's candle flickered on the white plastered walls as we listened to the murmured exchange below. Then Joseph called up.

"Elizabeth, bring the girls down. Our visitor has arrived."

Elizabeth's face was wreathed in smiles, and we all went to get shawls and went downstairs. And there in the hall with Joseph stood my father.

He held his arms out to us, and we ran to him and buried our faces against him and broke into tears. "There, there, children, we haven't time for this. I'm well and I hear your mother is, too. Come, come, we must catch up on news."

I looked up at him. "Father, I'm afraid," I said. "I'm afraid for you and for Mama."

"Not you, Susanna," he said. "You've never been afraid in your life."

"I have fears now, honored Father."

"We all do, child." He smiled at Joseph and Elizabeth. "When a knock comes on the door in the middle of the night, everyone in Salem trembles. Our forebears left their homes across the sea so we would not know such fear. And I've been in hiding for the past month to avoid arrest."

He held us close and kissed us. "This is not what I wanted in this land, for myself or my children. But I have come back now to face charges. This is not England. Persecution does not flourish here. This is

Massachusetts. People here are fair. So I have come back. Now, haven't you tea to offer me?"

In a short while, we were all sipping tea and talking at the board in the kitchen. Father ate ravenously of the meat and cheese and bread the Putnams had put before him. He told us of Boston, where he stayed with merchant friends. I listened to him tell Joseph and Elizabeth how Boston had joyously received Reverend Mather and Sir William Phips, though I did not care a king's shilling for either of them.

I just wanted to hear my father's voice again—the familiar tones, the learned words he used. I sat, as if under a spell, listening to him.

He leaned forward, his eyes gleaming. "I have heard there is already a schism amongst the judges who will sit on the Court of Oyer and Terminer. They worry the matter. Saltonstall does not believe in spectral evidence, and he urges caution. They say he thinks convictions should be on evidence more considerable."

"He is a man of good sense," Joseph said.

"You will accompany me when I turn myself in tomorrow, Joseph?"

"I will," Joseph said firmly. "But now my wife and I would leave you and the girls to your privacy. I know you have much to discuss."

When they had gone back upstairs, Father looked

at us. Except for some lines in his face that I had never noticed before, he seemed the same. There was but one change in him.

When he spoke, there were silences now between his sentences, as if he weighed every thought. It was as though a shadow fell over him, as if he had experienced some depth of moral isolation that would always be a part of him now.

"The Putnams are good people," he said. "Were it not for people like them, all of those accused would despair."

"They have made a home for us here, Father," Mary said.

"Your mother—Joseph says you see her once a week—how does she keep?"

"She stays busy helping others," I told him.

"Tomorrow I will turn myself in. They will examine me in court and accuse me of witchcraft. You must not come."

"Honored Father, please!" We both begged.

"No, you must stay here."

"How will I go with you to Boston?" Mary asked.

"Joseph has plans," he said. "Just wait to hear what he says and obey him. Susanna, are you sure you won't come with us to Boston? Your mother and I will be given our liberty during the day. The way matters have been moving, it will be a while before we come back here to go to trial. It has been three months since the naming of the first witches, and they have just set up a court to hear the first cases."

"I can't come, honored Father," I said.

"We will miss you, child. And I know how you love Boston. You can stay with Mary."

The very thought tempted me. But I could not let myself go, as much as I knew I would miss my family. I had to stay and speak out when the time came. "I will stay and wait for William," I said.

He patted my hand on the table. "The jails here and in Boston are overflowing with this witch business," he said sadly, "with new witches being named every day. And I hear now that there are rumors of witches in Andover."

"Andover? How can that be, Father?" I asked.

"Evil spreads," he told us, "ofttimes quicker than goodness. Now, I trust Joseph and Elizabeth or I would not allow you to stay, Susanna. But you made promises to your mother. I trust you to keep them."

I promised him I would, and we stayed talking until the first light streaks of day shone outside the window, until the birds stirred with their waking-up sounds. Ellen came into the kitchen, startled to see us there.

We had breakfast, and Father left for court with Joseph. That night when Joseph came home, it was late. Mary and I waited anxiously. Elizabeth had held supper for her husband. When we sat at the table to eat, he told us how matters had gone.

Father had appeared in court with dignity and grace to hear Susannah Sheldon testify that his specter had appeared to her and claimed to be God.

Oh, how that must have hurt my father! The judges reminded him of how his behavior on the Sabbath had been reprehensible, Joseph told us.

"Sometimes I think," Elizabeth said, "that those named as witches are always just a bit different from others."

Joseph nodded. "It would seem as such. It's as if the afflicted girls are being given instructions on whom to name to cleanse this society of dissenters."

"But who is giving such instructions?" Mary asked.

I looked at my plate. Who, indeed? Ann Putnam, the elder.

"Your father was brave, girls," Joseph said. "He asked the judges where was the religious toleration that people had come to this land to secure. And after it was over, we had a moment together before they took him away. He told me that someday, when this madness is spent, he intends to donate land for a church where he can worship as he wishes."

Mary and I looked at each other. Something was wrong.

"They took Father away?" Mary asked.

He saw the stricken look on our faces. Then he and Elizabeth exchanged glances.

"What about your plans?" Mary asked. "I thought I would be going to Boston with him?"

"Is something wrong, Joseph?" I asked.

"Let's finish our meal," he said. "Nothing is wrong. Let's finish our meal in peace."

It was the worst test of patience and good manners that Mary and I ever had. We would honor Joseph and keep silent, because we trusted him and knew by now that he liked order in his home. But Mary was white-faced, and I could scarcely swallow my food. We finished our meal in silence. Then the baby cried in her cradle, which was nearby, and I got up to fetch her. But Elizabeth put a restraining hand on my arm.

"You have other matters to attend to," she said.

Joseph stood up. "Are you packed, Mary?"

"Yes, sir."

"Then go get your cloaks, both of you."

I caught on immediately and felt my legs go weak. Mary was leaving now! But why must I get my cloak, too? "Oh, Joseph," I said, "you're not sending me away. Please! Have I done something to displease you?"

He hushed me. He came and put his arm around my shoulder. "Tell me," he said, "don't you wish to say a proper good-bye to your parents?"

Tears of relief came into my eyes. Mary had gone to fetch our cloaks and her bags. Joseph smiled at us.

"I have made arrangements. We bring Mary this night. You may come along, but only if you give me a promise."

"What promise, Joseph?"

"That you know, in your heart, it is good-bye only for a while, because you will be seeing your family again soon."

We drove through the night in an eerie silence that was broken only by the croaking of frogs and the evening songs of insects. As we neared the marshes, I heard two owls calling to each other. I fancied I saw shadows where there were none. I shivered in the wagon on the seat next to Mary. I held her hand and it came to me that we had arrived at a sad state of affairs here in Salem, that I must ride through the night like a thief to see my parents.

Even the night breezes seemed fraught with foreboding. The landscape all around Salem had become melancholy. And as Joseph's mare pulled the wagon swiftly over familiar paths, I felt as if we were all incarnated out of that melancholy, as if we were all part of it.

We met our parents under a tree at a bend in the road just past the marshes. They were waiting in their carriage. I immediately recognized their driver as

John Willard, a deputy constable who, in March, had brought in many witches. He held back in the shadows as Mary and I embraced our parents. Then, after they had shaken hands with Joseph, Willard told us we had only half an hour together. "I've put myself in danger, allowing this meeting," he growled.

I do not much ponder the farewell. But it still comes to the front of my mind at night when I hear owls calling to each other in the loneliness. Or when I catch the scent of the marshes. When that happens, I can still feel Mama's or Mary's arms around me, hear Mary's sobs as we drew apart, hear Father's voice break as it did when he tried to conceal his painful feelings.

I can, to this day, conjure up in an instant their whispered reassurances that we would soon meet again, the promises they wrung from me regarding my safety. Then it was over, and John Willard stepped out of the shadows and said it was time to go.

As they drove off into the night, I stood there feeling myself to be the most wretched person on the face of the earth.

"Come, Susanna." I felt Joseph's hand on my shoulder. I turned, reluctantly, from the receding carriage, the sight of which tugged and pulled at my heart. I will never see my parents again, I told myself. And who knows when I will again see Mary? I could not put the feeling from me all the way home.

18

HOW MANY MORE,
SUSANNA ENGLISH?

⟡. THE FIRST SES-
sion of the Court of Oyer and Terminer sat in Salem
on June 2 with all the pageantry Puritans could muster
and still be Puritans. There were the sounds of drums,
and constables and judges in wigs, looking for all the
world as if they were in Parliament in England.

All of this I heard from Joseph. Neither Johnathan
nor I went to court.

People in Salem were awaiting the trials. Those in
prison hoped to now have their names cleared. Joseph
said that John Proctor was amassing evidence on how
some of the men brought in were being chained heels
to neck to wring confessions from them.

The general feeling from those who opposed the

witch business was that such tortures should not go on in Massachusetts, that persecution could not happen in this new land.

But there were other people who awaited the trials eagerly, and the hangings they were speculating would follow.

Hangings? In Salem? Everyone waited to see what the Court of Oyer and Terminer would do.

As it turned out, it did little but go by the record of the previous hearings. The only new testimony they would consider was that collected since the accused was last examined. Then they let the jury deliberate. There were no new trials.

Bridget Bishop was the first case. Again she wore her red bodice into court. They denied her any counsel.

"They said the Devil was her counsel," Joseph told us. "The girls said her shape visited decent married men in their chambers at night. Deliverance Hobbs was there, and she, too, accused Bridget."

"Deliverance Hobbs?" I gasped. "Mother of Abigail?"

"Yes," Joseph said. "It seems she finds it more profitable to confess and implicate others."

"Tell us the outcome," Elizabeth said softly.

"They searched Bridget for a witch mark. The women said she had one. She is to hang," Joseph told us, "on the tenth of this month."

The whole of Salem Town and Salem Village went to see Bridget Bishop hanged on Gallows Hill.

Half the people were there because they believed she should hang. They held she had always been a troublemaker, putting aside God's ordinances in her manner of dress. And was she not defiant to women and flattering to their husbands?

Others went because they wanted to be there when the town fathers came to their senses and stopped the hanging.

I went with Joseph and Johnathan. We stayed a distance from the hanging tree. As high sheriff of Essex County, George Corwin presided. Reverend Parris came but said no prayer for poor Bridget, for she was not one of God's chosen.

And so, one of the marshals threw Bridget over his shoulder like a sack of potatoes, with a hood over her head. He carried her up the ladder, tied the rope around her neck, and threw her free.

I gave a small, muffled cry and turned to hide my face in Johnathan's shoulder. *They had started to hang people in Salem!*

"You should not come to these affairs henceforth, Susanna," Joseph said. "I shall forbid it. Your father would not want this."

Henceforth? Did he think there would be more such affairs in Salem, then?

"I must go to confer with friends," Joseph said. "Wait here for me."

We waited. The crowd was coming down the hill from the hanging tree, laughing and conversing as if they had just attended a husking bee. The afflicted girls sat on a stone fence a short distance from the tree, like crows lined up to observe.

"Notice how people do not go near them," Johnathan pointed out to me.

He was right. When the girls had arrived, people had stepped aside to let them pass, as if the ground, in a wide perimeter around them, was alive with fire.

A lone figure approached us, walking with the aid of a cane. It was Goody Bibber. I had not seen her since that day last winter when she advised me to seek entrance to the parsonage. "They call this place Salem," she said to us. "Know ye what that name means, Susanna English?"

When I did not reply, she answered with a cackle. "It means 'City of Peace.' "

Where had I heard this before? From Tituba, I recollected, that first day I went into the parsonage. Oh, it seemed so long ago! I drew closer to Johnathan. Goody Bibber watched us. There was a knowing light in her eyes but no malice that I could perceive.

"It's been a while since we last met, child."

I did not answer.

"Ye told me one day long ago that God reveals all things to us in His own time," she said. "What has He revealed to us this morning?"

"God has naught to do with what happened here," I said.

She nodded. "He has abandoned Salem."

"Salem has abandoned Him," I retorted.

"What do you want with Susanna?" Johnathan asked her. "You are one of the afflicted, are you not?"

"I am and I am not," she said. "They allow me around the edges of their circle. Never inside. I'm like John Dorich."

"John?" My eyes went wide. "John is one of the afflicted?"

"He is, poor lad. He's sat with them in court, where they let him tell, on occasion, of a vision. But they suck all the power from us. They don't allow us to be part of their dark fantasies."

"Who would want to be?" Johnathan asked.

"And why wouldn't one? No people in all of Massachusetts Bay Colony have such power. Aye."

"What do you want from us?" Johnathan asked.

"Susanna knows," she said softly. Then she turned and pointed to the lifeless figure on the end of the rope, etched against the blue June sky. "See how she swings in the breeze. Hear the creaking of the tree branch. How many others will swing on it, hey?"

"You're frightening Susanna," Johnathan said sternly. "Go back from whence you came. Go back to your friends."

"They're no friends of mine, lad."

"By your own admission, you're in league with them."

"Aye. But I've cast my lot with them because I choose to live. And not swing from a tree. I have no man, and that means no power. I'm poor, an old hag. No one listens to my mumblings. I'm sensible of such. I've no fancy to be cried out on. How many more do you think will swing from that tree, Susanna English?"

"I don't know." I buried my face in Johnathan's doublet. "Make her go away," I whispered.

"Go now, Goody Bibber, or I'll tell my father what you've said this day."

She cackled again. "And what is that, lad?"

"That you dissemble. To save your own skin."

"Many do, lad. Many do. Tell him and I'll deny it. He'll believe me. The magistrates have given us this power. How many more, Susanna English, hey?" And she burst into that cackling laugh of hers and moved away.

"She's a dafter," Johnathan said. "Don't let her bother you, Susanna. Joseph is right; henceforth you stay at home. And forget what she said. It has naught to do with you."

But I could not forget it. I went home and marked

it well. Goody Bibber was the only one now, except for me, who could tell the truth about the beginnings of the circle. And no one would listen to her, for she was poor and powerless and a crazy old hag.

She had appealed to me. How many more would swing from that tree before I stepped forward to tell the truth, she had asked.

I pleaded a sick headache that evening, which indeed I did have. Elizabeth put me to bed with warm broth and cold rags on my forehead. But whenever I closed my eyes, all I saw was Bridget Bishop swinging from that tree.

How many more, Susanna English, I now asked myself. But how could I speak out? From April 21 until May 12, Mary Warren had attempted to speak out. And no one would listen to her until she reverted back to her original lying testimony. Then they cleansed her of her sin.

Almost at the same time, Sarah Churchill defected from the circle. After her master, George Jacobs, was accused, she became frightened and tried to discredit the lies of the afflicted girls, who then named her a witch. What followed was now accepted. No one could believe the testimony of a named witch. So Sarah recanted and was taken back into the circle.

In my throbbing head, however, one thought persisted: I have Joseph and Elizabeth. They will believe me.

As if by some predestined sign then, Elizabeth came into the room to give me to drink of bitter potion. It soothed my head and made me sleepy. And just before I fell off to sleep, I made my decision. I will go in the morning to Joseph. I will tell him what I know. I finally fell asleep in peace.

But in the morning I did not do it.

I slept late. Elizabeth had not wakened me, and I came into the sunny kitchen, where Ellen gave me a large breakfast. Elizabeth was nursing the baby.

"Where is Joseph?" I asked.

"Gone off to a meeting. You know how secretive he is. He'll tell us when he returns."

Joseph came back midafternoon. "Good news," he said, taking a mug of ale from Elizabeth and removing his doublet. "Saltonstall has resigned from the Court of Oyer and Terminer."

"Resigned?" Elizabeth could not believe it. Neither could I.

"Your father was right, Susanna. There is division amongst the judges. My information is that Saltonstall objected to the haste with which Bridget Bishop was convicted and executed. He is against spectral evidence. My information is that he said she was hanged because she wore a red bodice."

Silence in the kitchen. Joseph reached for bread and meat. "There will be a delay now until the court sits again. The judges are in an uproar, looking to the ministers now for reinforcement. But the public is not to know of it."

"The ministers started all this," Elizabeth noted.

"Aye," Joseph agreed. "All is confusion. I'll wager we'll not see another witch hanging in Salem for a while."

And so I did not speak out. I waited to see what would happen. After all, I told myself, if the wisest men in the colony were confused and needed time, so then, didn't I?

The lovely days of June passed. On the fifteenth, twelve learned and holy ministers met in Boston, not the least of whom was Reverend Cotton Mather. They decided that care was to be exercised in regard to spectral evidence, "lest by too much credulity for things received only upon the Devil's authority there be a door opened for a long train of miserable consequences."

In other words, if one of the afflicted girls said that someone's shape had visited her to do mischief, such evidence weighed less than before. I rejoiced at the news. Surely, now, no more people would be condemned.

The court sat again on June 28, in Salem Town, not Salem Village. Mayhem prevailed. The girls were at the height of their powers, and their howls could be heard up and down the street outside.

Rebecca Nurse, Elizabeth How, Sarah Good, Sarah Wild, and Susanna Martin were tried that day.

The girls charged Susanna Martin with bewitching John Allen's cattle so they ran out to sea and drowned. At Sarah Good's trial, young Ann Putnam wrestled with an invisible knife at her breast. Then she said the specter of Elizabeth How had stuck needles into her hand. Another afflicted girl said that Sarah Wild had overturned people's hay wagons and sent demons to fly out against them.

All the accused pleaded innocent.

But the judges paid no heed to the document recently issued in Boston by the ministers. They condemned all the accused to hang on July 19.

Once again, no one believed the hangings would take place. They would not dare to hang Rebecca Nurse! I must speak out, I told myself. But then Joseph went with the kinsmen of Rebecca to Boston to see Governor Phips in her behalf. And they had a meeting with the governor, who was having an interim stay in that town.

They came back with a reprieve from the governor for Rebecca Nurse. I breathed easier. Rebecca was safe for now. Yet I must still approach Joseph or the others would hang.

But he was back only a few hours before he was off again. He'd come home at two in the morning from Boston, Elizabeth told me at breakfast, so she was allowing him his sleep. When he awoke I would speak to him, I decided. Then a rider came to the house with news, and Elizabeth had to wake him.

Somehow, the Devil had been loosed in the town of Andover. Joseph was needed there.

The wife of one Joseph Ballard took sick and Ballard sent to Salem Village to summon two of the afflicted girls, the messenger told Elizabeth.

So Joseph packed to go to Andover to try to put down the panic. I could not speak with him that morning.

But the townsfolk of Andover did not want the panic put down. They welcomed young Ann Putnam and Mary Walcott, offering them every comfort and want. Ann and Mary were asked to visit many sickrooms. Needless to say, in every household they saw witches, though they could name none. How could they? They did not know the names of the citizens of Andover.

Such details did not bother the good people of that town, however. Before Ann and Mary were finished there, forty warrants were written out for the arrest of witches. Who would dare speak out against the testimony of the afflicted girls?

Dudley Bradstreet, the justice of the peace, for one. After signing the forty warrants, he announced himself done with the witch business. The girls cried out on him, and he fled to New Hampshire with his brother John, who was also named.

Reverend Francis Dane, for another, with whom Joseph was staying, begged his parishioners to listen to reason.

Elizabeth and I saw Joseph's hand in all of this.

As a matter of fact, everyone in Salem was so concerned by what was going on in Andover that they scarcely paid mind to the fact that July 19 was fast approaching.

And then more unfortunate news came to us. Governor Phips had also granted an audience to the proponents of witchcraft, who told him that devils had brought sickness to some of the afflicted girls in Salem. Indeed, they told the governor, some of the girls were dying. And they had said that the devils had come in the name of Rebecca Nurse.

So the governor made void his reprieve for Rebecca.

July 19 was but a few days away, and I waited, feverishly, for the return of Joseph from Andover. I peered out of windows constantly, looking for his carriage down the road. I walked to the end of his property line and stood by the gate by the hour. But no Joseph came.

I was in a state of near-hysteria on the morning of the nineteenth. Elizabeth saw my affliction and put it down to concern for my parents, so she said nothing when I harnessed Molasses to the cart and rode off.

In my little cart I sat a distance from Gallows Hill, but not so far away that I could not see the figures carried up the ladder and hanged.

I could not tell one figure from another, but I did not have to. I counted them. Rebecca Nurse, Susannah Martin, Elizabeth How, Sarah Good, and Sarah Wild. One by one the hangmen carried them, bound hand and foot, up the ladder, put hoods over their heads, ropes around their necks, and swung them free.

I was sick at heart.

Joseph came home in the early hours of the following morning. I put a shawl around me when I heard him come into the house, and I went downstairs. He was in the kitchen, at the table, half leaning over it, drinking something from a mug.

He looked bleary-eyed and discouraged and exhausted.

"Joseph," I said.

"Yes, Susanna." He looked up at me. His face was lined with the pain and terror of all that had transpired.

"I would speak with you, Joseph."

"I am weary, Susanna. Is it important?"

"It is very important, Joseph."

He met my eyes, and I saw the dark shadows under his own, saw the day's worth of stubble on his face, the smoky gray intensity of his eyes, and I could have sworn he knew what I was about to say. "Very well, Susanna," he said. "Come and sit."

19

My Dark Tale

🌿 JOSEPH HAD taken off his doublet when he came in. It was over the back of a chair. As I took my seat at the table, he loosened his waistcoat and collar.

"What matter is so serious that it cannot wait until first light, Susanna?" he asked. "Concern for your parents? They are faring well in Boston."

I decided to get directly to the heart of the matter. "I have not been worthy of your friendship, Joseph. Or of Elizabeth's."

"You have been a friend to Elizabeth as well as a help," he assured me. "She would have suffered much loneliness these past weeks, with my being away so much. And this day, after a few hours' sleep, I must be off to Boston to a prayer meeting at John Alden's. After which I meet with Nathaniel Cary, who is trying to have his wife's trial changed to Suffolk County. I tell you this in strictest confidence."

"I will honor your confidence, Joseph. But you must honor mine."

He leaned forward with interest. Candlelight played across his handsome face. "Speak, then," he said. "What besets you, to have you roaming the house at this hour?"

"Joseph, I have not been honest with you."

His countenance did not betray any surprise. He nodded and gestured with a strong, capable hand that I should continue.

"The afflicted girls dissemble, Joseph."

"We are sensible of that, Susanna, those of us who have managed to retain our sense in Salem. But we have no proof."

"I have proof."

He raised his eyebrows. "Then tell me, child."

"Joseph, I know not how to start."

"At the beginning. There is always a beginning, Susanna. Of every mysterious happening and calamitous event. Ofttimes, it is very simple."

"The beginning goes back to last December."

He nodded and waited for me to proceed. I took a deep breath and did so. "There was a circle, Joseph. All the afflicted girls belonged to it before the madness began. They would meet every day at the Reverend Parris's parsonage. It was for sport."

"Sport?"

"Yes. They met with Tituba. She told them stories, read their palms, and conjured."

"Conjured?"

Such a word, from the lips of that practical and decent man, sounded unnatural in that kitchen. "There are things hidden, Joseph, that I know of. I fear telling you."

"Have I given you reason to fear me, Susanna?"

"No."

"I thought there was trust between us."

"There was. There still is. But I have not told you everything."

"Then tell me now."

"Very well, Joseph. I wanted to join the circle. They seemed to be having such good times. But they didn't want me. Then I heard that Tituba was telling fortunes. And I went to see her without the knowledge of the girls in the circle. I wanted to know if she could tell me of my brother, William, who was then lost to us, at sea."

He smiled ruefully. "Sometimes I wish there were someone I could seek out who would tell me what lies in the future. Go on, Susanna."

"On my first visit, Tituba told me William would return. On my second visit, I met little Betty Parris.

She was taken with the fever that would lead to her fits. She was near demented and raving about how I would be punished if the other girls found me there. And how she had tampered with the forbidden. Oh, she was a frightened and guilty little thing, Joseph! She said her father preached against forbidden pleasures, and she indulged in them. Soon after that, her fits progressed and Reverend Parris summoned the doctor."

"And he pronounced the evil hand upon her."

"Yes."

"Are you saying there was a connection between her fear and guilt and her fits?"

"Yes, Joseph."

"Do you know this to be so?"

"Yes."

"Tell me how you know such."

"Once the ministers pronounced her afflicted and the other girls began to behave in kind, I became suspicious. I went to visit Ann Putnam, who was the leader of the circle almost since the beginning."

"You speak of my niece?"

"Yes."

He leaned back in the chair, arranging his long limbs as if to position himself, physically, to ward off whatever I might tell him next. But nothing in his manner was in the least unfriendly to me.

"She admitted everything to me on that first visit, Joseph," I said softly. "She said they had started the circle for sport, then little Betty was torn with guilt and became sickly. And Abigail Williams behaved in kind, because Betty was getting so much attention. Then, when the ministers came, the rest of the girls in the circle became afflicted in like manner, because this was their chance. I understood immediately what they were about."

"Excuse me, Susanna, I do not understand. Their chance for what?"

"To break out of the restrictions put upon them by our way of life in Salem. No one condemned their behavior when they went into fits. Everyone hung on their every word. They were coddled and no longer had to do chores or go to Meeting. They could act out all their wishes, and no one would stop them."

He nodded silently.

"Ann Putnam told me that little Betty and Abigail did not have the sense to carry the matter through without being discovered. So she and some of the other girls met with Betty and Abigail to explain how they must continue to outwit their elders or be terribly punished. Ann said they swore fidelity to each other and promised to give succor to one another until the end."

"And you told no one of this at the time?"

"I couldn't, Joseph."

"Why?"

"Ann Putnam threatened me."

"How?"

"The ministers were soon to question them and ask the names of their tormentors. She said she would name my family as witches, if I told what I knew."

"Go on," he whispered hoarsely. In the dimness of the candle-lit room, I could see the look in his eyes and how this was causing him pain.

"I kept my silence. They named the first three witches. Then Mama was arrested, and I went to see Ann Putnam again. She said Mama had sealed her own fate by standing up for Sarah Cloyce and my silence could no longer protect her. But she reminded me that they could name my father or Mary. Or brother William, when he returned. I was frightened, Joseph. I kept my silence."

"But she named your father."

"When I saw Ann after Mama's arrest, there was a change in her. She was filled with a power. She said they were carrying out the Lord's charges and giving the ministers what they wanted by naming witches. I saw she had started believing her own lies. And though Father had escaped to Boston with Mary, I knew authorities were searching for him there. I still had much to fear."

"You were living with us by then. Didn't you

know I was working with others against the witch-craft?"

"Yes, Joseph. And I wanted to tell you—oh, I did! But there was Mary Warren, trying to tell what she knew—and no one would believe her. And then nobody thought Bridget Bishop would hang. No one ever thought they would start executing people in Salem!"

"But they did, didn't they?" His voice dropped to a whisper.

"Yes. And then Sarah Churchill defected from the circle and tried to tell what *she* knew. But no one believed her, either."

"She tried to tell the *magistrates*. She did not try to tell *me*. She did not have *me* to confide in, Susanna. You did."

I sensed his growing anger, as well as his pain.

"After Bridget Bishop was hanged, I was determined to tell you, Joseph. I stayed awake all night, pondering it. Then you came home and told us Saltonstall had quit the court. Everyone had hope. So I waited. Then the ministers in Boston came out with their document against spectral evidence. So, when the court sat again at the end of June, we thought no one would be accused."

"But they were." He got up and walked to the window and stood looking out. Lightning was flashing on the horizon. The air was cool in the early morning hours, but the day would be another scorching one if it did not rain. There had been a drought, and we were all praying for rain.

"Yes. I wanted to tell you when they condemned Rebecca Nurse and the others. But you went to Boston with Rebecca's kinsmen and came back with a reprieve."

"Only for Rebecca." He turned to face me, and his face was dark with disapproval. "What of the others who were condemned with Rebecca?"

I felt myself going weak under his anger. "I intended to tell you when you returned from Boston. But in a few hours you were off to Andover. The nineteenth and the executions were approaching."

I put my elbows on the table and hid my face in my hands. "I waited for you to come home, Joseph. Down by the gate. I prayed for the sight of your carriage. Then Governor Phips took back his reprieve, and they hanged Rebecca and the others. I went to that hanging."

I raised my eyes to look at him. He scowled in reproach. "I had to go. I became sick at heart. Then you came home this day. And now I have come to you."

He said nothing. The silence in the kitchen stretched out like a frazzled rope that barely kept me attached to my sanity.

He turned to gaze out the window again. "We'll have rain this day," he commented.

I waited.

"Between the drought and the way people have been ignoring their crops, it will be a bad winter in Salem. Many will go hungry."

I did not know what he expected me to say. Why did he speak of such matters now?

"You saw me running, day and night, from here to court, to people's houses, to secret meetings, to Boston and to Andover, trying to make some sense out of this whole dark tale, Susanna," he said finally. "You could have come to me."

He turned to fasten his gaze upon me. I looked at him mutely.

"You knew I was working with people like Reverend Wise of Ipswich and Reverend Hale of Beverly. And Reverend Dane of Andover. You knew of John Proctor's petition begging for his life and the lives of others. You knew of John Alden, who comes from one of New England's foremost families, imprisoned in his own home. And you said nothing."

"I was afraid, Joseph," I said tremulously.

"Do you fancy we are not? Do you think John Proctor is not afraid? Yet he stands up to them. Did you not think Rebecca Nurse was afraid when she went to the gallows? Yet she acted with dignity and faith, even when they put the noose around her neck. She refused to confess to witchcraft, though those who confess are not hanged and those who do not confess are."

"Joseph, please." I started to weep quietly.

"What of Robert Calef of Boston? The girls cried out on him because he spoke out against them. He has responded by asking a thousand pounds for their acts of defamation."

I wept quietly under his angry words.

He sighed. "Right now, fifty people languish in prison in Andover on the word of the girls. Well over a hundred are imprisoned elsewhere. And some are dead. I would have honored your confidence, Susanna, had you come to me. Did you not trust me, after all?"

"Forgive me, Joseph," I said. "I was so confused and frightened. I wanted to tell you so many times, and something always happened to prevent it. Determine that I am silly or stupid. Anything. But don't accuse me of not trusting you. I have admired and trusted you so for what you are doing."

His stony silence persisted. I stood up. "I will leave your home, Joseph, if you wish."

His scowl became even more forbidding. "Did I say I wished such?"

"No. But I cannot stay under your roof if you cannot forgive me."

He shook his head, still scowling. "There is no time for this now. Sit down."

"But, Joseph, I cannot stay if . . ."

"We *cannot* allow ourselves such feelings—I, my anger, or you, your self-pity. You have come to me now. I expressed my anger at what I perceived to be your lack of trust. You say such was not the case. Very well, I choose to believe you. I will put my anger aside and ask you to forgive it. And to please sit, or you will see anger unleashed that you have heretofore not witnessed."

I sat. He did, too. But first he went to the hearth, picked up the kettle, and brewed some tea. "We have much to talk about," he said.

And so we went over the whole matter again. We exhumed the bones of it and picked them clean, going over every fragment of detail, lest we miss something.

Then he pondered a while. Weary though he was, his mind was that of a scholar's. "Have you told Johnathan of what you know?"

"No. I would not dishonor you by telling him first, Joseph."

"Good. I would have you not tell him. Or Elizabeth. For their own protection. I must decide how best to use your information. The timing must be right. Up until now, no one in any position of importance in Massachusetts Bay Colony has come out against the trials. Until someone does, all our meetings and petitions will come to naught. We *must* get someone in authority to speak out. I have lain awake nights pondering on how that can be done. Now we have *this* to lay at someone's feet. But whose?"

I said nothing. He smiled. "It must be the right person at the right time. And when that time comes, Susanna, you must agree to come with me and tell what you know. Will you do that?"

"Yes, Joseph."

"I will stand by you. You must not be afraid. This is a brave land, Susanna, founded by brave people who never shrank from their duty or their vision of freedom. But this land has a future only if each of us stands up for what is right when it is given us to do so. Now go to bed, child; you look spent."

I was in the hallway when he called out to me. "Susanna, come with us to John Alden's today. We leave at eight."

20

THE WITCH ON THE WINDLASS

WHEN I WENT down to breakfast later that morning, I found Johnathan at the kitchen table, deep in conversation with Joseph.

"Johnathan brings us good news," Joseph told me. "Magistrate Corwin is having doubts. He is weakening."

I sat down to eat. Magistrate Corwin had taken Saltonstall's place on the Court of Oyer and Terminer when Saltonstall resigned. I stared at them both. Perhaps it was too early for me to feel any joy at such news. What did it mean? And how could Joseph look so wide awake after being up half the night?

"We've been talking here for two hours," Johnathan told me.

"Didn't you get any sleep, Joseph?" Elizabeth came into the kitchen, yawning, with Mary in her arms. "She's been fretting all night. I think she's cutting teeth. Joseph, I'll have to beg off going to Alden's this day. It looks like rain, and the baby is feverish. And my own body groans with lack of sleep."

"I shall miss your company," Joseph said, "but these two young people will accompany me."

I watched him reach across to Elizabeth and pat her shoulder; then he took Mary and balanced the baby on his knee. How did the man do it, I wondered. He was freshly shaven. He wore a clean shirt and waistcoat. He looked more bright-eyed than any of us.

"Have you heard, Elizabeth?" he asked her. "Johnathan's father has told him that Corwin is having doubts. It's the occasion we've been waiting for."

"Yes, but Corwin will never give public voice to those doubts," Elizabeth predicted. "The man is too fearful."

Joseph ate his breakfast while he jostled baby Mary on his lap. His brow was furrowed, and he chewed slowly. "If I could push him along a bit, move him . . ."

"And how could such be done?" Elizabeth asked,

as she poured her tea. "The man won't even speak with you."

"True, but he'd speak with Magistrate Richard Pike of Salisbury. These magistrates always give succor to one another."

"Joseph, you are plotting." Elizabeth laughed. "Tell us, so we can help."

"When Saltonstall resigned from the bench, Pike rode over here to see why," Joseph said. "And when people came to Pike in Salisbury, to give depositions about Susanna Martin when she was accused, he made several remarks indicating he was against the whole business."

"And don't forget," Johnathan intoned, "that Pike has been called a heretic for standing up for Mary Bradbury. He testified to her charity and piety."

"Who is Mary Bradbury?" I asked.

"She is accused of witchcraft," Joseph explained. "She has been married fifty years and has eleven children."

"Is that the same Mary Bradbury who has the butter business?" Elizabeth inquired.

"The same," Joseph said. "You are right, Johnathan; Pike came out strongly in her defense. He does not seem to mind being called a heretic. He is the one who must get to Corwin. I must ponder on how to bring this about."

"Corwin is upset because his mother-in-law, in Boston, was cried out on by the girls," Johnathan said.

"That's right," Joseph said. "We have that in our favor."

"Was she arrested?" Elizabeth asked.

"No," Joseph answered. He and Elizabeth started to discuss the matter.

"Mary Bradbury was accused of haunting ships at sea," Johnathan told me. Then he fell silent. Everyone did.

I felt my face go white.

"If there is something I should know, please tell me," I said.

Johnathan looked to Joseph, as if for permission, and Joseph nodded solemnly. Johnathan explained. "Sam Endicott, a Boston shipowner, testified against Mary Bradbury. He lost a ship that had just left Barbados. In a storm. He said he saw her on the windlass, cackling at him as the ship went down. The rest of the story is silly and deserves no attention."

"Tell me," I said.

"Oh, very well." Johnathan sighed. "Sam Endicott claims Mary Bradbury boasted of leading pirates to the *William and Susanna*. And of haunting many Massachusetts Bay ships in the Caribbean."

I felt a sense of dread overwhelm me. "Where," I asked, "is this Sam Endicott now?"

"In Boston," Johnathan said.

"Can you take me to see him this day?"

He and Joseph exchanged looks again. "No," Joseph said. He got to his feet and handed the baby back to Elizabeth. "We have much to do, and you should not give credence to such gossip, Susanna. I am also making arrangements to bring your parents to Alden's after the prayer meeting. You won't have time to run around looking for Endicott."

"But, Joseph—" I started to protest.

He scowled down at me. His face was flushed with some of the anger I had borne witness to earlier this morning. "Don't you want to see your parents? And would you give me argument, when I have much to concern me?"

I did not know whether to answer yes or no. So I said nothing.

"Finish your breakfast if you would come with us," he said gruffly. "I must gather my things."

I ate. Elizabeth jostled Mary on her shoulder. "Don't pay heed to Joseph," she said. "Lack of sleep has made him boorish."

"I pay no heed," I said. But to myself I made a promise. I would see Endicott this day. I would prevail upon Johnathan to take me to him.

We made the trip to Boston in good time. Joseph kept his twin bays at a swift pace to make the ten o'clock ferry. As we rode around the Lynn marshes, the skies, already overcast and brooding, threatened to open upon us at any moment. But the rain held off, and we were able to get out of our carriage on the ferry to get benefit of the breezes in Boston Harbor.

Johnathan and Joseph were deep in conversation as they stood near the horses' heads on the ferry. I could scarcely get two words in with Johnathan.

It was hot in Boston, but the town's rhythms seemed different from Salem's. There was a gaiety everywhere, whereas in Salem people avoided each other on the streets, ducking their heads and going about their business like frightened crows, intent upon not attracting attention.

It was hot, too, in John Alden's frame house, which was filled with people. They were assembled in the company room for prayers. I had never met Alden, but like every young girl in Massachusetts Bay Colony, I had heard much of his exploits as a sea captain and a famed Indian fighter. I looked forward to meeting him. Wouldn't my sister, Mary, love to meet him, too, I decided. Perhaps she would have the opportunity later.

The room was filled with all manner of persons, lowly and distinguished. Joseph moved through the crowd slowly, greeting them in soft tones. All about the walls and on the chests were curios from Alden's adventures—Indian artifacts and other treasures from around the world.

A sudden hush came over the room as Alden entered. He stood by the hearth to welcome everyone. He was a tall man—very tall—and lean. His eyes were deep set and his movements cautious, like a cat's. He was well muscled, and his strong-jawed face was browned. He wore a soldier's rough clothing: leather breeches and doublet, rough shirt, and woolen stockings.

"Good and gentle people," he said in a voice that was at once kind and strong, "the tall man from Boston welcomes you and thanks you for coming to pray with him."

There was a murmur of appreciation that this man could have any humor left in him. For his accusers had identified him as "the tall man from Boston," echoing Tituba's words for the Devil.

"Where is your black hat, John?" someone asked.

"I have sold it to the Indians along with some powder and shot."

Soft laughter. But Reverend Cotton Mather scowled. Not yet thirty, the younger Mather, whom my father had called a dunderhead, was dressed all in black. He wore a wig and looked like the very incarnation of evil, rather than a man of God. I heard him whisper to Judge Sam Sewall that Alden was irreverent and in need of prayers. Then Mather began to pray in a great and thundering voice.

The praying lasted nearly an hour. Halfway through, a rumbling of thunder sounded, lightning flashed in a most fearful manner, and the room grew dark. Then the downpour came. Rain! After weeks of drought. Mather paused and acknowledged the rain, acting as if his prayers had brought it on. Alden's maidservant went about lighting candles. As I watched her move through the kneeling figures, Joseph came over to whisper something in Johnathan's ear, then slipped out a side door.

In the kitchen, after prayers, cakes and cold cider and ale were laid out. As the others moved back into the company room with food and drink in hand to hear Judge Sewall read a sermon, I put a hand on Johnathan's arm.

"Stay a moment."

"Gladly. I have no desire to hear Sewall preach. We've scarce had time to ourselves. Joseph means well, but he often keeps us apart."

"You're one to complain. You spend all your time talking with him."

He smiled, but I saw the hurt in his eyes. His smile, the even white teeth, made him seem so innocent, and I was reminded how attracted I was to him. "Where has Joseph gone?" I asked.

He shrugged. "He doesn't tell me everything. Nor do you, Susanna. Sometimes I think you have more secrets with him than I have conversations."

"What secrets could I have with Joseph?"

"I don't know. But there are times I feel you are keeping something from me. And you look up to him so and are so anxious to do his bidding."

"I am living under the man's roof. I must show respect."

"You worship him, Susanna. Anyone can see that."

"Are you accusing me of being his jade? Like Mary Warren was John Proctor's?"

"No, Susanna, I know you too well. And I know Joseph."

"You worship him no less."

"Aye. He's been part father and part adviser to me since my father removed himself from that responsibility. He has those qualities of leadership that attract loyalty. . . . Let's not quarrel, Susanna. Our time together is scarce."

"I don't do Joseph's every bidding, Johnathan," I insisted.

"Nor do I."

"Prove it to me, then."

"How?"

"Take me to see Sam Endicott. I would see him today. You know where he is to be found. You know everything to do with the trials, and he's a witness."

He shook his head in wonderment. "You mean to go now?"

"This very minute," I said.

"It's raining. We have no transportation. And Joseph told me, before he went on his strange mission, that later on today he's having your parents and sister brought here."

"At what hour?"

"Five this afternoon."

"We can rent a carriage. And be back by then."

"Susanna, why must you see this man? Joseph won't like it."

I sipped my cider and set down the mug. "Now who's following Joseph's every command?" I moved toward the company room. He grabbed my wrist and looked down at me with those blue eyes of his. A lock of his curly hair fell over his forehead, and I went weak.

"I'll take you, Susanna. Though I indulge you and will get into trouble for it."

Johnathan hailed a carriage, and we drove down to the wharves, through winding streets, past the marketplace, past the Town House, where the General Court sat, past elegant brick houses, silversmith shops, taverns, countinghouses, and, finally at the wharves, shops sporting the wares brought in by ships from all over the world.

The street was crowded with carts and carriages, rowdy young boys, sailors from distant shores, and women of ill repute.

"Joseph will have me hanged if he finds I took you here," Johnathan mumbled. We got out of the carriage. The rain had stopped, and the cobblestones glistened. As I turned to the waterfront, I saw rows of ships at anchor and men unloading goods, hawking wares in carts, and just loitering about. Gulls cried overhead. My eyes filled with the sights, my nose with the rich sea smells.

Overhead, a sign that said Endicott Shipping creaked in the breeze. Johnathan guided me with a firm hand under my elbow as we skirted some sailors and went through the door.

A blackamoor fetched Mr. Endicott from a back room. The shipowner was my father's age, well dressed, but limping and using a cane.

"How can I help you two young people?" he asked.

Johnathan explained who we were. Sam Endicott knew my father, of course, and shook his head in bewilderment to hear my parents had been accused of witchcraft. "All of the Bay Colony seems to be in the

Devil's grip these days," he said. "Everywhere you look, you see the Devil's minions."

"My parents are no minions of the Devil, sir," I said.

"There is no doubt, child, that some are innocent. But they have the chance to clear their names at the trials. Sit, both of you."

We sat. His blackamoor brought a tray of tea and cakes.

"What do you wish to know, Susanna English?" he said.

"They say you are accusing Mary Bradbury of being a witch."

"Aye. She's every inch a witch, child."

"Do you have proof?"

He sipped his mug of ale and regarded me with eyes so old, eyes that had seen so much, that his words were as afterthoughts to what I saw in them.

"I lost two firkins of butter because of her on one occasion. On another, I lost a ship. She has the powers. She made restitution on the butter when I demanded it but muttered curses at me as I left. Then, when I was in the Caribbean on my next voyage, those curses worked her evil. My ship was ripped apart during a storm."

"How can you blame her?"

"I saw her likeness with my own eyes, child. Right

in the middle of that storm. First I saw a cat on board. We had no cat, yet there it sat on the windlass. Then, before my eyes, it became the shape of Mary Bradbury, cackling at me while my ship ripped apart."

Outside, sheets of rain came again, tearing against the windows. Mr. Endicott leaned forward.

"We were just out of Barbados, and the sea was calm. The storm came up at dusk, from out of nowhere. My ship, the *Good Intent*, was sturdy. but it was a vengeful storm. I lost the mainmast. Waves swept over us, throwing the *Good Intent* on her side and my crew into the sea. Most swam back to the wreck, myself included, though my right leg was smashed. All night the storm wreaked havoc with the *Good Intent* while we clung to her. And in the midst of it I looked up and saw Mary Bradbury, her clothing as dry and spotless as if she sat at Meeting."

"Could not the ravages of the storm have made you delirious?"

He set down his mug and picked up his pipe and began to fill it, but he never took those old and weary eyes from me. "Lass, when you've been at sea as long as I, you see all manner of strange things. Pirates, sea monsters, boiling waters in the middle of the ocean, drownings, murders, duels on board, haunted galleons that sail by with no crew on moonless nights, floating bodies that appear out of nowhere on the calmest of waters. And, yes, witches on the windlass. For a sea captain not to believe what he sees, invites trouble. Ask your brother when he returns."

"You say Mary Bradbury boasted to you of leading pirates to the *William and Susanna*," I pressed.

"Aye, lass, she did."

"When?"

"When I spoke with her a fortnight ago. She's in Arnold's Jail here in Boston, awaiting trial. She said mine wasn't the only vessel she destroyed. And indeed, her demonic activities are well known amongst Massachusetts Bay Colony seamen."

"Then why do they have dealings with her?"

"They fear buying their butter from anyone else, as do I. With her own tongue she told me . . ." Here he broke off and looked at Johnathan. " 'Tis not a seemly matter to let fall on a young girl's ears," he said.

"Tell me," I insisted. "If it's about my brother, I must know."

"Aye, lass. She said she would avenge herself on William English by causing harm to the *Amiable Tiger* on its voyage home."

"The *Amiable Tiger?*"

"Aye, lass. It's the forty-five-ton schooner recently out of Guadeloupe, bound for Massachusetts Bay Colony. Your brother is on it."

I felt a surge of joy, quickly benumbed by fear. "How come you to know William is on this ship?"

"Mary Bradbury told me."

"How does she come by such knowledge?"

He shrugged and puffed his pipe. He did not answer, but his eyes said all he would not put into words.

"Why does she wish to avenge my brother?"

"That is the unseemly part, but you would have me say it. Many a witch visits a man in his chamber at night. Witches are seducers of men. She told me young William English would not have her when she visited him in his cabin on the *William and Susanna*."

I looked at Johnathan. He was shaking his head. "We should take our leave, Susanna. It is late."

"Yes." Numbly I got to my feet and thanked Mr. Endicott.

" 'Twas a pleasure, lass. We'll have that witch condemned, never you worry. She'll visit your brother no more on his ship. Or sit on anyone else's windlass."

"You don't believe his tale, do you, Susanna?" Johnathan asked me in the carriage on the ride back to John Alden's.

"He believes it," I said.

"He's a seaman. He fears tempting fate. If *you* believe it, you'll be like so many others in Salem, believing in witches."

I sank back in the seat as we raced through Boston's

winding streets in the rain. My head was spinning. Johnathan was right, I decided, there are no witches. And for me to believe Sam Endicott would mean I, too, would be swallowed up in the witch madness.

But it was so easy to be drawn into it when one of your own was threatened! And hadn't Mary Bradbury threatened William's return voyage? How did she, living in Salisbury, know the name of the schooner he was returning on unless she was a witch?

My feelings were betraying me. Were there, indeed, witches? I knew by now that certain people had powers. Tituba had them. Hadn't she predicted that I would see the ship of clouds?

Did some people have special powers for good and other people have them for evil? Did such special powers make people witches? Had the actions of the girls in the circle, innocent enough in the beginning, simply opened a door through which witches had entered?

Oh, I did not know, I did not know! I knew nothing anymore, it seemed. All reason had fled. But through my confusion, one thought pushed its way, like a haunted galleon through a wall of fog.

I could not tell the truth about the girls in the circle until William safely returned. I must let the witch trials continue. Mary Bradbury must go to trial. Certainly, she would be condemned. I could not take the chance and let her live. Or William might be destroyed.

And then, just as I had made my decision, as if struck by some unseen hand, our carriage seemed to drop to the ground and come to a grinding halt. Johnathan and I were tossed about inside. I hit my head on something and I heard the driver yell in an attempt to halt the horse.

For a moment, I went unconscious. When I became sensible again, Johnathan was patting my hand and calling my name.

"Susanna, are you all right?"

"What happened?" I was on the floor, looking up at him.

He helped me onto the seat. "I think we broke a wheel."

"Oh, Johnathan!"

"Stay here. I'll get out and confer with the driver."

21

A PROMISE IN MOONLIGHT

✵ THE NIGHT
watch was crying the hour when we arrived back at
Alden's. Eight o'clock. It had taken us three hours to
repair the carriage. The driver had had to send to a
wheelwright on the other side of town for a new
wheel. We arrived at Alden's wet and hungry, and
my head hurt. Joseph awaited us in the empty company room.

I was in a fevered pitch of anxiety, hoping my
parents and sister had waited for us. But they were
nowhere in sight.

Joseph stood, grim and white of face, his arms
folded across his chest. "It is good of you to make an
appearance this evening," he said coldly. His blue

eyes were frosty and veiled over with a mist of anger.

"Our carriage wheel broke," Johnathan explained. "Or we would have been here three hours ago."

"And where did you go in this carriage? Or need I not ask?"

I spoke up. "It isn't Johnathan's fault, Joseph. Don't blame him. I prevailed upon him to take me to see Sam Endicott."

"Don't tell me where to direct my anger, please. I will direct it at whomever I wish."

We stood like naughty children before him. I searched the rooms beyond us, hoping against all hope that my parents and sister would appear any moment, that he had them hidden in the kitchen, perhaps. He saw me casting my gaze about.

"Your family was here and gone," he said coldly. "Your parents had to be back in Arnold's Jail by dusk. But first they had to take Mary back to her lodgings."

I choked back a sob but to no avail. The burden of the whole afternoon had been too much for me. *I had missed my family. And they had waited for me.* Oh, I could not bear it. I began to weep openly. Johnathan took my hand.

"I went through great pains to transport your family here," Joseph said. "On an afternoon when I had much else to do."

"I'm sorry, Joseph," I said. Johnathan murmured

his apology, also, but Joseph dismissed our words and brushed past us to the door.

"You owe such words to your family," he said. "They dearly wished to see you. Come along, we must catch the ferry."

John Alden came into the room then. "There is food in the kitchen. Don't you want some before your journey?"

But I had lost all appetite. I said no and thanked him. He smiled at me kindly. "I met your family. They are good people. My house is open to all of you if you wish to stay the night. Then you could see them tomorrow."

"Oh, could we, Joseph, please?" I begged.

"Thank you," he said to Alden, "but I must get home to Elizabeth and the babe. We never know, hour to hour, if we will be the next accused. I have been gone too long already. I say come now, you two. The ferry does not dally."

We arrived home near midnight. Joseph had not spoken to us all the way. I fell into bed, exhausted. Johnathan stayed the night but was gone in the morning. I woke to a blue sky, clear air, and an earth washed by rain. But Joseph's silence was still oppressive. And after breakfast, he summoned me to his library and closed the door.

I prepared myself for another scolding, praying I

would have the mettle to stand up to him. But he spoke with sadness and kindness instead.

"Susanna, I met with Reverend Moody yesterday, as well as with your parents. He will call on your mother and father at the end of this week and invite them to public worship in his church. The text of his sermon will be, 'If they persecute you in one city, flee to another.' "

I tried to understand. Clearly, he was readying me for some grievous news.

"After the service, Moody will invite them and your sister to dine in his home, as he has done so graciously over these past few weeks. He will then convince your parents not to come back to Salem for their trial but to flee instead."

"When are they due in Salem for trial?"

"Monday next. Your father wants to stand before the judges, because to flee from trial would be the same as if he were convicted. He knows they can then seize his property and he must forfeit it. And your father is a man of much wealth. It will be Moody's job to convince your father that there will be no justice for him back in Salem. The good reverend and I have provided a means of escape for your family. They will stay with merchant friends in New York."

I understood then what he was telling me. "I will not see them again, will I?"

"Not for a while, Susanna, no."

I started to cry, quietly. He did not change his expression, but neither did he utter words of recrimination. "You will see them someday," he said kindly.

"Take me back to Boston, Joseph," I begged.

"Only if you wish to go to New York with them, Susanna. It is too dangerous otherwise. None of this is pleasurable for me. Don't think I take satisfaction from your misery. Johnathan told me last night why you went to see Sam Endicott. He also said you tend to believe the man's story. Do you?"

"I don't know what I believe anymore," I said.

"Well, I do," he said. "And I know I can get Magistrate Pike to put quill to paper and write to Magistrate Corwin. If we tell Pike what we both now know."

I stared at him. What was he saying?

"I have written to Pike, inviting him to the trials here in Salem the first week in August. George Jacobs, Martha Carrier, George Burroughs, John and Elizabeth Proctor, and John Willard come to trial then."

"Willard?" I asked. "The deputy constable who drove my parents to Boston?"

He smiled ruefully. "Yes. He came back from that trip to tell the magistrates of the wrongness of their doings, that he would bring in no more friends or neighbors, and that they should hang the afflicted girls for witches. The girls cried out on him."

I pondered this in silence.

"When Pike comes in August, Susanna, I would have you tell him what you know about the circle."

I looked out the window, saying nothing.

"Your family will be safe in New York by then. But we must prevent the execution of others."

I continued to gaze outside. A morning breeze lifted the leaves of the trees. I heard the floorboards creak as Joseph came to stand beside me.

"You will do it, won't you, Susanna?"

I looked up into his face, which I had come to know and love as one would love a father's or brother's. "Oh, Joseph, I can't. Please forgive me." And I burst into a fresh onslaught of tears and ran from the room.

Over the next fortnight, I did not know where to fasten my misery. On my foolishness for missing my parents' visit at Alden's house or on the fact that I was hurting Joseph.

Within this time, Joseph handed me a letter from my parents. They had escaped and were on their way to New York with Mary and were faring well.

He looked at me as he handed me the letter. "You must now expect your father's belongings to be confiscated, Susanna," he said. "He has made provisions for the servants."

Joseph gave me my peace, never once chiding me about refusing to speak to Pike when he came to

Salem in August. He continued to treat me with quiet courtesy. But whenever his eyes met mine, I saw in them the burden of what I was doing to him.

I began to wish I had never come to stay with him and Elizabeth. They were like kin to me now. I had brought disorder into their household. Such a thing was unforgivable.

I took many walks in the meadows. I wandered down the path to the gate to await Johnathan. Over and over in my head on these walks, I reviewed the facts. Sam Endicott had visited Mary Bradbury in prison. She told him William was on the *Amiable Tiger*, bound for home. My parents had said in their letter that they'd heard nothing from William, but that Mama prayed for him daily.

At night they were in Arnold's Jail in Boston, where Mary Bradbury was. If Mary Bradbury knew such, why hadn't she told Mama that William was coming home?

Because she intended William harm, that was why.

Round and round, these thoughts danced in my head. Day and night. I barely ate. Dark circles appeared under my eyes.

Johnathan noticed something was wrong. One evening after he had supped with us, we were walking in the meadow.

"I know you have argued with Joseph," he said. "But Joseph scolded me, too, for taking you to see

Endicott. Yet he and I are friends again. Don't hold grudges, Susanna."

"It isn't that, Johnathan."

"What, then? You heard that Sheriff Corwin confiscated your father's house and belongings?"

I stopped short. "I knew that was going to happen. I didn't know when. Has it?"

He blushed. "I shouldn't have told you. Yes. I'm sorry, Susanna."

Tears came to my eyes. "It isn't your fault, Johnathan. I had to know sooner or later. Joseph and Elizabeth must have been keeping it from me."

"But if you didn't *know* of it, then that isn't what's plaguing you. What *is* then?"

"It's what Endicott said. I believe him, Johnathan." I told him my reasoning. I could share that misery with him without divulging what I knew about the circle. He listened solemnly. And we discussed the matter of Endicott again. We talked until the first stars appeared, until Joseph beckoned in the distance with a lantern that we should come in.

Then Johnathan held me as insects chirped all around us.

"I love you, Susanna English," he said. "Do you feel in kind about me?"

"Yes, Johnathan. You are the only good thing that has happened to me in this unfortunate time and place."

"It is a bad time," he agreed. "But the madness will pass and our love will continue. Still, I cannot stand to see you torn apart."

I buried my face against his chest. Poor Johnathan. He sensed something terrible was tormenting me. And I was hurting him by not sharing my anguish with him.

"I wish we could run from this place, Johnathan," I said. "And never have to do with this witch madness again."

"We can't. We who know better must take a stand for what is right. And bring our community together again."

Joseph had said such words. That this country had a future only if each of us stood up for what was right.

"I don't know what ravages you, Susanna," Johnathan was saying. "But I can try to help you on one score."

"How?"

"Mary Bradbury is scheduled to come back to Salem for trial. We who work with Joseph know she will be condemned. We have planned her escape, just like we planned your parents' escape. And we will help John Alden run away when the time comes."

I pulled away from him. "She is a *witch*, Johnathan."

"She is an old and feeble woman. No more a witch than any of the others."

"A *witch*," I said again. "You must not help her escape!"

"Susanna, you are trembling." He held me close. "Oh, Susanna, do you trust me?"

"Of course I do."

"Did I not prove my love by taking you to see Sam Endicott, wrong though I was to do it?"

"Yes."

"Then prove yours for me by listening now."

I listened. His voice was low and soothing, but firm. "Fear and distrust are what caused this witchcraft menace in Salem. Those who can remain untouched by it can see it for what it is. But you have been touched, Susanna, by fear and mistrust, with this story about Mary Bradbury harming William. You scoffed at the idea of witches before. But now the specter of Mary Bradbury has taken you down a dark road."

"You know what Sam said."

"I know that you now have reason to accuse Mary Bradbury of witchcraft. Because you think she can do you harm."

"I have good reason."

"Many felt Bridget Bishop's red bodice was good reason. Ann Putnam, the elder, thought her dead sister's children were good reason."

"Am I like those others, then?" I looked up into his dear face.

"Fear renders us all foolish, Susanna. It takes all substance from our thoughts and leaves us grappling with illusion. I will allay your fears for you."

"How?"

"Joseph and I, and others, have it planned. I am to go to my father and offer to bring Mary from Arnold's Jail in Boston to Salem for her trial. They are short of deputy constables, now that John Willard is in prison. My father will be glad of the help. Our plan is that instead of taking her to Salem Prison, I am to meet with others who will help her escape, then tell my father we were ambushed. But now I embellish the plan to help you."

"How?"

"I will stop the carriage at Gallows Hill. You will be waiting there for us. You will meet with Mary Bradbury."

I gasped. "Johnathan, I dare not!"

"And why? I will be there. She is naught but a helpless old woman. When you meet with her and witness her good nature, you will know her not for a witch."

"You have met her?"

"I went with Joseph to Arnold's Jail to meet with her and plan her escape. She shines with an inner light, Susanna. Like Rebecca Nurse did. I would have you see that light. To deflect your darkest fears."

In the gathering dusk, he smiled down at me.

"Love and trust me, Susanna. Give reason a chance, lest you go down that dark road, no more to return."

"Oh, Johnathan!" I could not resist him. His love wrapped around me like a mantle of protection. I succumbed to it, for this was true power, true magic.

"Well, am I to take this ardor for agreement?"

"Yes, Johnathan, yes!" Tears streamed down my face. For he knew nothing of my misery, yet had seen my terror. And because he loved me, he hoped to restore me to myself. He did not know it, of course, but in doing this he might well give me back the courage to speak out about the circle and save many other lives.

All he did know was that he loved me. And that was enough, after all. Love was all any of us needed to slash away at the hidden specters haunting us in Salem. For love was what was lacking in this place, and now Johnathan was offering it to me. And I could not refuse.

22

UNDER THE HANGING TREE

  AND SO IT WAS that I found myself one night, the last week in July, under the hanging tree on Gallows Hill, waiting for the sound of carriage wheels on the road below.

The moon was almost full and gave good light. Not far from where I stood with Molasses's nose nuzzling my shoulder, the ropes dangled from the tree. And the ladder leaned against it.

Johnathan was late. My eyes searched the road below. I was three miles from Joseph's house. Overhead an owl hooted. All around me I fancied I saw shapes. A warm and gusting wind fanned down from the north, stirring the trees with an unworldly sound. Above my head, the leaves of the great old oak hanging tree turned upward so that their undersides appeared silver.

The ride here in my little cart had been terrifying. The wind had banged the shutters on Reverend Parris's house as I took the road around Thorndike Hill. It had rustled cornstalks in Dr. John Endicott's meadow, played havoc with the underbrush in the open stretches between the houses of Sarah Phillips and Joseph Buxton, and swayed treetops so they assumed long arms that seemed ready to reach down and pluck me away.

I felt abandoned, alone in the world. What were those figures across the road? Deer come to graze on the sweet grasses? Raccoons come to gape through masked eyes at the frightful hanging tree? Or the spirits of Bridget Bishop and Rebecca Nurse, dancing on the wet ground?

If Johnathan did not come soon, I decided, I would lose my senses and run from this place. I sat down, drew my cloak around me, and waited. I thought of my mother and father and Mary safe in New York. Someday we would all be together again, Joseph had promised me. Someday I might even travel to New York. It was inhabited mostly by people of Dutch descent whose heads were filled with figures of profit from business ventures and not with fears of witches.

Just then I heard the distinct sound of carriage wheels on the road. I stood up and peered across the moonlit landscape. Yes, there it was. I could hear the labored breathing of the horses. I ran down the hill. In a moment, the carriage drew up and Johnathan alighted from the driver's seat and helped a woman down.

"Susanna?" His lantern threw a friendly beam to cut the dark. And above it I saw his dear face.

"I'm here, Johnathan." I ran to him and hugged him. "Oh, Johnathan, I was so afraid. I thought you weren't coming. I fancied those deer across the way were spirits."

" 'Tis a night full of shadows and images. I wouldn't blame any young girl for not wanting to venture out. But were I your age, I'd come out in a blizzard to meet a young man like this," a voice said.

I could not see her face, for the hood of her cloak covered it. She stood next to Johnathan, a small, frail figure.

"Susanna," Johnathan said, "this is Mary Bradbury. This is your witch of the windlass."

As if it were midday, we sat on the grasses beneath the hanging tree. Johnathan set his lantern in the middle of our tiny circle, and it afforded enough light to see Mary Bradbury's face.

"Hello, Susanna English," she said. And she smiled at me. "Ah, Johnathan, I see ye have chosen well."

Her smile, as Johnathan had said, was warm and

without deceit. And her eyes sparkled with girlish delights and secrets, in spite of the wrinkled face.

"Johnathan told me how Sam Endicott put an ancient fear into you, dear. The old goat. If he imbibed a little less rum, he might not have seen witches on his windlass." Her smile broadened. "I met your parents in Arnold's Jail. Your dear mother gave such comfort to me as to make my stay there bearable. D'ye think she did not hear the accusations against me? That I was accused of bringing pirates to the *William and Susanna*?"

"Mama knew this?"

"Aye, child." She nodded gravely. "And she paid it no heed. Never believed it for a moment."

"Did you tell my mother that William is coming home on the *Amiable Tiger*? And that you would destroy the schooner before it reached here?"

She laughed, a girlish sound, like the tinkling of a bell. "Child, how would I know what ship your brother is coming home on? And why would I wish to destroy him? I've known William since he was a little lad. Your father would bring him to my place when he purchased his butter to ship out."

"My father has done business with you?"

"For as long as he's been a merchant."

"I never heard your name spoken in our house."

"D'ye know how many business ventures your father was involved in? D'ye know all the names? Have ye perused his ledgers?"

"No."

"D'ye think me a witch, then, child?" It was said in such sadness that I felt compelled to meet those bright eyes, which were now filled with remorse.

I did not answer.

She took my hand. "D'ye think I was indeed the witch on the windlass of Sam Endicott's ship? Child, let me tell ye, 'twas always my secret fancy to go to sea. I wished myself on every ship that left Salem Harbor. How I longed to be a man and visit such far-off places as they spoke of! But I tell ye now, were I a witch, I wouldn't plant myself on some old windlass. I'd be up there in the crow's nest seeing the world from that lofty height!"

I smiled, for her vigor and dancing eyes invited such a response.

"The windlass, bah!" And she pushed aside the thought with a slender hand. "I'd be up there in the crow's nest, feeling the salt spray on my face and sighting the sails of other ships on the horizon. Haven't ye ever wanted to go across the Atlantic Ocean, child?"

"Yes." She had touched on my innermost fancy, and I found myself confiding in her. "Someday my brother, William, will take me."

"Go, child. Go with him. Don't care what they

say. Go while ye are young enough, if ye have the opportunity," she urged.

"Let me show Susanna the petition, Mary," Johnathan said.

"Not yet, lad. I've another matter to bring forth." And she leaned toward me. "Were I a witch, would I bother to meet ye on a hill on such a windy, forlorn night, after journeying from Boston? I'm weak and grieved now from my stay in jail. My old bones yearn to be abed, but I have more traveling to do yet this night."

Her voice dropped to a whisper. "Child, there be no witches. Believe me. There is only an old woman before ye who has borne and raised eleven children and been married fifty years to Thomas Bradbury. Mayhap I needed special powers to survive all I've been through, but that makes me no witch."

"It's getting late, Mary," Johnathan persisted. "We must rendezvous with our friends. The petition will convince Susanna."

"Lad, if such were so, ye could have taken the petition from your father's papers and shown her. No, I want this child to behold me, Mary Bradbury, frail and old as I am. I want her to look into my eyes and heart and see that I am no witch. Though Ann Putnam herself avowed that her kinsman Richard Carr saw me turn myself into a blue boar and dash myself at the feet of his horse."

"Ann Putnam, the daughter?" I asked.

"Nay, the mother. She lived in Salisbury when young; I've known her a long time. And believe me, were I to turn into a boar, it wouldn't be blue. It would be a lovely bright red. Oh, how I've always loved the color red. And I'd dash myself at Ann Putnam, troublemaker that she be, not at her kinsman."

I smiled.

"Aye, child." She nodded. "And someday the ministers and magistrates will be apprised of the fact that those named as witches are all within the circle of Goodwife Ann Putnam's acquaintances."

The words, spoken with such clarity of heart, raised my spirits. But still my mind was not at rest, though I wanted so to believe her.

Sensible of my confusion, she took my hand again. "Look into my eyes, Susanna English."

I looked.

"See ye any sign of alliance with Satan?"

"No. But I would not know such if it were there."

"Ye would know it, child. Believe me. Does my touch afflict ye?"

"No."

"There are no witches, child. They exist only in the Puritan heart. The ancestors of these people hereabouts came to this land with a vision of a godly society. They came to escape the past. What they

254

quickly discovered is that the nature of man and woman is such that sin can flourish here as well as from whence they came. What they do not yet understand is that the spirit it took to tame this wilderness is so strong it would not bow to the authority of the Puritan covenant and its ministers. So strong that it will always question authority. They see this not as something to celebrate, but as a failure of their vision. So they seek to lay blame."

Her logic made wonderful sense. Her words sounded like something my father would say. And they lighted the gloomy night around us as much as the glow from Johnathan's lantern.

"Thank you," I said. "For your wisdom and for coming this night."

" 'Twas worth the trip, child, to see your heart lifted. Now you may show her the petition, Johnathan."

He unrolled the parchment. "Here ninety-three neighbors have put their names," he said, "to declare that in half a century in the town of Salisbury, Mary Bradbury has never been known to make trouble, that she is a devout woman, a good wife of Thomas, and mother of eleven upstanding children."

I let my eyes wander over the petition. When I again raised them to Mary, she smiled at me. Tears slid down my face. I embraced her.

"Forgive me," I said.

Her slender arms gripped me in joy and forgiveness. Then we parted. We went down the hill from the hanging tree. Johnathan helped Mary up into the carriage. "The crow's nest, child," she said before they drove away. "When your brother takes you to sea, climb the mast to the crow's nest. Do it for me."

I promised her I would. Then they drove away. And I was alone in the windy night.

But the hooting of the owl was friendly as I turned my cart toward home. The rustlings of cornstalks in Dr. Endicott's meadow were murmurings of encouragement. The swaying treetops now seemed to be loving arms guiding me on. And the warm wind dried the tears on my face as I drove away from that long dark road in my soul.

23

THE TIME HAS COME

SUN FILTERED through the windows into the Putnam kitchen and shone off the polished wood of the table. There Joseph, Johnathan, and I sat and watched Reverend Richard Pike of Salisbury as he wrote his sweeping sentences on the parchment in front of him.

Through the open door came the sounds of a cow lowing in a nearby pasture, the calling of crows from a tree, the chirping of insects singing the praises of that hot August day. From another part of the house came the becalming singing of Elizabeth as she put baby Mary down for her nap.

Reverend Pike halted in his writing to take a sip of cold cider. A bee buzzed around the pitcher on the table. Joseph waved the bee away. The reverend drank the cool liquid, wiped his mouth with a clean square of cloth, then blew his nose.

"I'm more beset by goldenrod than by the specters of witches," he said.

Joseph smiled.

"If the Devil is anywhere in Massachusetts, he's out there in those fields, where grows the cursed weed that makes a man so miserable," Pike went on. He blew his nose again and set back to his task.

We waited anxiously as the scratching of his quill pen went on and on. When finally he set the pen down, he looked across the table at me. "Susanna English," he said.

"Yes, Reverend."

"Stand, child."

I pushed back my chair and stood.

"Are ye sure, Susanna English," he intoned in his best preaching voice, "that everything you have told me here, this seventh day of August in the year of our Lord sixteen hundred and ninety-two, is true?"

"Yes, Reverend, I am sure."

"Do ye attest to these words of yours as being spoken truly from the heart and the mind, with no intent to do damage to others, but only to speak truth?"

"Yes, Reverend."

"And ye will not recant later?"

"I'll not recant, Reverend."

"Nor have second thoughts?"

"I have had all my second thoughts, Reverend. And more. I am done with my doubts now."

He nodded and waved his hand. "Sit, child, sit." Then he handed the letter to Joseph, who took a few moments to read it while we waited. A furrow appeared on Joseph's brow.

" 'Tis a wonderful letter, Reverend. I especially like the part where you say that proof of witchcraft is dark and uncertain and confession often necessitated. And that under these circumstances it is safer to leave a guilty person alive until further discovery than to put an innocent person to death. But you have mentioned nothing that Susanna told you."

"The magistrates and ministers have had more than enough observations from young girls," Pike said. "They need no more. But I say this now: I would not have put pen to paper today had this young girl not told me her tale."

Joseph nodded. "You protect her name. I appreciate this. But you have signed the letter with only your initials."

"Magistrate Corwin knows from whence it comes. The time is not yet upon us for signing lone names on parchment. This is but a start. Let us pray now that this one letter, written on your gracious board, will give others the courage to speak out."

Joseph smiled. "One person of courage writing a

lone letter on a kitchen table can change the world. Thank you, Reverend."

Pike nodded and regarded me with his rheumy, red-rimmed eyes. "You've done us all a great service, lass. Thank ye."

"Thank you," I said.

Joseph walked him outside to his horse.

"How fare you now, Susanna English?" Johnathan asked me.

I smiled up at him. "I fare well, Johnathan, but I didn't think it would be this way. All these months, when I fancied myself telling authorities what I knew, I saw myself standing in a courtroom before men in long robes and white wigs. I saw rain slashing on the windows, and the girls rolling on the floor."

"How you must have suffered, Susanna." His words were tender, his touch as he drew me toward him equally so. "And I never sensible of what you carried in your heart until you told me yesterday."

"I couldn't have spoken out today, Johnathan, if you hadn't brought Mary Bradbury to me."

We stood close together. "I'm glad that I could do something for you. I knew not what troubled you, Susanna. Only that I love you and wanted to help."

And there in Joseph's kitchen, we kissed. It seemed so natural, kissing in the kitchen like an old married couple. In the next moment came the sound of Joseph clearing his throat. We looked up. He stood in the doorway. We drew apart.

The golden sun framed Joseph. And as I looked at him, in his breeches and summer shirt with the sleeves rolled up, as I beheld the slender strength of him, I felt a surge of love for this plain and decent man who had fought so hard for all the accused. Who had not pushed or berated me to speak, but waited patiently for me to do so.

I ran to him and he hugged me. "Thank you," he said.

"Will the letter help, Joseph?" I asked.

"It's a beginning." He smiled at us both. "It will take time, but it's a beginning."

It took time. And it took more lives.

On August 19, they hanged George Jacobs, Martha Carrier, George Burroughs, John Proctor, and John Willard on Gallows Hill.

The Reverend Cotton Mather came from Boston for those hangings. Joseph told us, at supper, how Mather rode up on his great dark horse, dressed all in black from head to foot. And he sat there etched against the hard blue August sky like death itself.

The crowd became disgruntled, Joseph said, because Burroughs recited the Lord's Prayer before he was hanged. It was common knowledge that no witch could recite the Lord's Prayer without making a mistake.

Cotton Mather raised himself in his stirrups then and told the people that the Devil sat on Burroughs's shoulder, whispering in his ear. Then he rode away while the mutterings of the crowd continued.

"What of Reverend Pike's letter?" I asked. "Has he sent it to no one?"

"To Magistrate Corwin," Joseph said.

"And does Corwin do nothing?" Elizabeth asked.

"We have one good sign, wife. No one is arresting Corwin's mother-in-law in Boston, and the girls are constantly crying out on her."

"So Corwin rushes to save his mother-in-law," I said bitterly, "while others hang."

"A man speaks out cautiously these days, Susanna. The fact that his mother-in-law has not been arrested weakens the position of the girls. That may be the only contribution Corwin can make right now. But it is a good one. And Pike is showing the others. I cannot name them now. Be patient."

On September 19, they took Giles Cory into an open field and pressed him to death by setting large stones on a board on his chest. Giles had refused to testify in court. For if he did not testify, if he were not found guilty, they could not seize his worldly goods.

Joseph had tears in his eyes as he dismounted his

horse and told me about Giles. "All he said was, 'More weight,' as they piled the stones on." Joseph looked around the yard. "It is difficult to believe such things are happening in this peaceful land. Giles fought them to the end. Now his family gets his land and his goods."

"My speaking out was for naught," I said sadly.

"No," Joseph said. "We must go to Boston within the week to see Thomas Brattle. He wrote to me that he was much moved by Reverend Pike's letter. You see, Susanna, Pike has been showing it to others."

"I have heard this Thomas Brattle's name before," I recollected.

"He is held in great esteem," Joseph said. "He is about to become treasurer of Harvard College. And he would meet with you to hear from your own lips what you told Pike. You must tell your story again, Susanna. This is a man who will sign his full name to any document he writes. Where is Elizabeth?"

"Bathing the baby."

"I must tell her to get ready for the trip."

From the windows of Thomas Brattle's parlor, one could look out to the Charles River, where the masts of tall ships floated past red, gold, and russet trees along the banks. The sky was a cloudless blue. When I pulled my gaze from the scene, I could fill my eyes with Brattle's richly furnished room.

Carpets imported from Turkey covered polished wood floors. Heavy wood wainscoting decorated the walls. Beautifully bound books were lined neatly on shelves. Velvet draperies hung from the windows. Next to a glowing hearth, Elizabeth and I took tea served from a silver pot by a maidservant.

At his intricately carved desk, Brattle poured his best Madeira. One crystal glass for Joseph, one for himself.

All around the room was evidence of this man's full life. There were curios from around the world, astronomy equipment, leather-bound ledgers, a jade chess set, and silver candlesticks in profusion. Brattle himself wore a brocaded waistcoat and breeches of soft material. He seemed to know Joseph well. And he'd taken Elizabeth's hand and kissed it in the European manner, then mine.

"It is so good to meet the daughter of Phillip English, a friend and fellow merchant," he said. "Bring your teacup to my desk, child. Have another cake. Don't be anxious. I shall honor your confidence. I long to hear what you have to tell me now."

And so I told my tale once again, to that kind and learned man. At first I *was* anxious. After all, he was a world-traveled merchant, astronomer, and mathematician.

And when I started to talk, my words seemed so out of place in this well-appointed room. I felt my tale had no merit, that my words were the ramblings of one from some backwater place bereft of civilization.

But his interest never waned. He took notes as I spoke. And I took heart from the sight of Elizabeth and Joseph and baby Mary sitting across the room from me.

Even as I told my story on that day, September 22, back in Salem they were taking Martha Cory, Margaret Scot, Mary Esty, Alice Park, Ann Pudeator, Wilmott Red, Sam Wardwell, and Mary Parker to Gallows Hill, where they hanged them until they were dead.

"I will write a letter," Thomas Brattle said when I stopped talking. He got up and paced before the windows. "I have wanted to write such a letter for weeks now. The trials are a sham. Oh, shameful, shameful, what has transpired in Salem! The evidence is based on common gossip! I scorn these magistrates and these lying she-brats. I sensed the girls were pretending from the outset. Now that I hear what this child tells me, I know my instincts are right."

"To whom will you send such a letter?" Joseph asked.

"I shall address it, 'Dear Sir.' "

"Will you publish it?" Joseph asked.

"No, I shall have copies passed from hand to hand, in lieu of publication. Let us pray that enough men of goodwill have the brains to come forth now and speak out."

We went home to Salem and waited. We resumed our lives. In the fortnight that followed, I looked back to my visit to Boston as if it were a dream.

I did not know anymore what was real and what I had dreamed. I felt as if I were a ship without anchor, floating toward some distant harbor, not knowing what to expect when I got there.

I woke every night when everyone was asleep, afraid. I found myself afraid most of the time. It was as if a hand was put upon me to wake me from my dreams, which were always bad and had nothing to do with anything I recognized, except in the feelings of terror that pervaded them.

I would lie in bed plunged into depths of fear that I had heretofore never known existed. I would think of my family and yearn for those wonderful days of my past when we were together. I asked myself what had happened to us all and how could such things happen to good people. And why did I never realize how precious those days were that went before. I knew my life would never be the same, and I wondered if we would ever be happy again, any of us in Salem.

By daylight, however, I was cheered. As autumn colored the landscape with the sun still warm in the afternoons, as I took baby Mary out for a walk or helped Elizabeth make cider from the apples in Joseph's orchard, I knew in my heart that the world would be right again. Autumn has always renewed me. And that year I had the additional good feeling of knowing that if life in Salem were ever to be good again, I had had a part in making it so.

But side by side with that thought was the guilt I felt at realizing that people might be alive if I had spoken out sooner. I could not enjoy one feeling without suffering the other. And so, when the witch madness ended, finally, like everyone else in Salem I was left with self-recriminations, which stay with me always.

On October 9, Joseph came racing up the path toward the house, waving a piece of parchment in his hand.

"Brattle's letter! I have a copy!"

It had been released the day before, and Brattle had sent one by special messenger to Joseph.

"A copy has gone to Governor Phips," Joseph told us breathlessly. "It was on his desk when he returned to Boston the other day. Word is that Phips is going to write to the Privy Council in London. He returned from his recent trip to find Boston in an uproar from the impact of Brattle's letter!"

We hugged each other, Elizabeth and Joseph and I, with baby Mary between us. Tears streamed down my face.

Three days later, Johnathan dismounted his horse at the front gate and came through the door while we sat at supper.

He stood there, benumbed. We stared up at him. "Governor Phips has written to the Privy Council in London," he said, "informing them that he is forbidding further imprisonment on the charge of witchcraft."

Silence in the kitchen. We just stared at him. The only sound was that of baby Mary gurgling in her own little language.

It was over. I felt a strange floating sensation. Silently, with subdued rejoicing, we hugged each other, and Johnathan sat down with us to eat.

I cannot speak for the others, but for me there were more guests in that kitchen than Johnathan. They were the spirits of those hanged.

They numbered nineteen persons.

On October 29, two memorable events occurred in my life.

My brother, William, came home, and Governor Phips dissolved the Court of Oyer and Terminer.

Over 150 persons still languished in prisons, but Phips had all the children released, as well as those adults jailed only on spectral evidence. And petitions were pouring in to magistrates in Topsfield, Glouces-ter, Haverhill, Chelmsford, and Andover, from people urging the release of their kinsmen.

Winter was coming. "There will be more trials," Joseph predicted. "But never again will they be as before. Phips cannot just empty all the prisons. He needs time, but his eyes have been opened. I'll wager that by spring he'll come to his senses completely and pardon all who remain in prison."

We had been expecting William, for a letter had come the previous week from the captain of a ship put in at Salem Harbor, telling us of the imminent arrival of the schooner William was due to come in on.

The letter was addressed to our parents. It had gone to Magistrate Hathorne, who had Johnathan deliver it to us.

The air was cool and crisp as Joseph, Elizabeth, little Mary, Johnathan, and I drove to Salem Harbor. We waited on the wharf, in the midst of people, boxes, crates of goods, carriages, and the usual may-hem, for William's schooner, which was late.

The masts of several small ships were etched

against the fine blue sky. My heart was beating wildly. Johnathan held my hand.

"You are cold," he said.

"Yes."

"And trembling."

"Will he know me?" I asked. "How do I tell him about our parents? He will expect them to be here. He will find no family here but me."

"He will find us with you," Joseph said.

"How can I even begin to explain to him what has happened in Salem in his absence?"

"After pirates and imprisonment, William will be able to abide it," Joseph predicted.

I could scarce keep myself from falling apart as the schooner docked. My eyes scanned its decks, the men coming down its gangplank. *Where was he?*

And then, in the next moment, he was there, standing taller than I had remembered, his face and hands browned from the sun, the growth of a fortnight's beard on his handsome face, a pipe in his mouth. I saw him looking around for familiar faces. "William! Oh, William! Over here," I called.

Joseph pushed me forward. "Go to him," he said.

I ran. I saw recognition come upon William's face. The pipe came out of his mouth. The eyes, so accustomed to searching the sea's horizon for pirate ships, squinted in the bright sun. "Susanna?" he asked. "Is it you?"

"Oh, William!" And I ran to him. He set down his bags and swooped me up in his strong arms. And as he whirled me around, I saw through my tears the name of the schooner he had journeyed home on.

It was the *Amiable Tiger*.

Epilogue
1706

Mulling over the whole matter as I sit in church waiting for Ann Putnam to appear, I mind how painful it is to recollect the events of those days. But once we allow memory to open its floodgates, we are hard put to stop its flow.

I stayed with the Putnams all that winter of 1692 and 1693. 'Twas brother William's wish, I recall now. Though he chose to live in our house on English Street while he oversaw its repair.

Only one piece of furniture, a servant's bed, remained in our house. William slept in it, amongst the ruins. I went once or twice a week to give my advice about the draperies, carpets, and furniture he was importing from England so as to have the house ready for our parents' return.

In November, right after William returned, the General Court of the colony created the Superior Court to hear the remaining witchcraft cases. In this court the justices traveled to try each witch in his or her own county. And spectral evidence was no longer allowed.

Yes, they still condemned witches, but Phips would not allow anyone else to be executed.

William joined forces with Joseph's people, who were now working with Phips to bring weight on the justices to have the condemned reprieved.

Joseph and William were of like mind and took to each other immediately. William often supped with us, and the Putnam house became a meeting place again for those working for the release of prisoners.

That winter there was dire want in Salem, for crops had been sadly neglected, and the farms of many of the accused were abandoned. William immediately wrote to Father in New York about the matter. And Father looked about him and saw the full corncribs and warehouses and sent hundreds of barrels of corn and flour to Salem to help feed his neighbors.

Some of these things I have not thought about in years. It all seems so long ago now. Oh, I sit here and I smile at some of it, and yet I also wish to cry.

In May of 1693, Governor Phips pardoned everyone still in prison for witchcraft. But John Alden had long since escaped to Duxbury, and Mary Bradbury was safe in Connecticut.

My parents came home in June, on a day when the world was alive with blossoms and the air was like silk. A great crowd of people came out to meet them in the road. Mama told us later that she had become frightened. "Oh, Phillip," she had said. "Do they come to arrest us again?"

The crowd was led by Judge Hathorne, Johnathan's father. In his hands he held the silver goblet Mother had given Father the day they met. It had been confiscated with Father's other things.

Mama was not well. Prison had made her ill, ruined her health. She died the following winter of consumption.

My sister, Mary, married Thomas Hitchbourne. They live here in Salem. I married Johnathan in 1697. In the summer of 1694, William took me on a sea voyage to Guadeloupe, where he was traveling to meet and bring home his beloved Juliette, whom he had met there while in prison. She is the daughter of the French magistrate who invited him to dinner.

I was the only woman on board on the outward bound voyage, and was very coddled. One fine day, I dressed in some of William's clothes and climbed up the mainmast to the crow's nest.

As I peered out across the calm waters, with the salt spray in my face and the wind blowing my hair, I whispered softly, "This is for you, Mary Bradbury. I do this for you."

William was very upset when he saw me up there, of course. And he scolded. But I was happy. How many young women get the opportunity to do such a thing, after all? I shall forever be able to close my eyes and feel the salt spray on my face. It was worth the scolding.

"Perhaps, if you go and stand with your neighbors, you will manage to forget," Johnathan told me before I came here today.

Forget? I think I never will. Nor will the others assembled here now. How can we ever forget how the community was torn asunder, how smashed and ruined houses of some accused were left to the wind and the wolves. How businesses went bad because outsiders refused to have dealings with those in Salem for years afterward.

How can I forget how Father acted when Sheriff George Corwin died ten years ago? Father near lost his mind. My honored Father, a gentle and decent man, seized the body of Corwin and would not release it. He could not forget that Corwin had set himself on his wharves and warehouses, his ships at anchor in the harbor, as well as his home and Mama's shop. Nothing we said at the time could convince him to release Corwin's body. Not even William could reason with him. Mary and I feared he was going mad.

He did release it, finally, when Corwin's heirs agreed to some restitution. But the nightmare of that time has never left me. And Father still dislikes Johnathan's father for his part in the witch trials. They barely speak two words to each other at family gatherings, and this is hard for Johnathan and me to bear.

But in so many ways, Father is still generous and kind. Look how he donated the land to have an English church built in Salem. It will be called St. Peter's. Yes, there are still those who would have him ousted from this community for wanting an English church. But Father says this country was founded for freedom. And that should include freedom of worship.

When I dwell on all that has happened, I could myself go mad, but I must not dwell on it, for I must be a good mother to my own children.

Look there, now! Here come the kinsmen of those who were hanged. Oh, there is the Widow Preston, daughter of Rebecca Nurse. And John Tarbell, Rebecca's son-in-law. There are her other sons and daughters and their wives and children.

So many of Rebecca Nurse's children. Such a large and wonderful family. There are the kinsmen of Martha and Giles Cory. And all of John and Elizabeth Proctor's children. And Sarah Cloyce, sister to Rebecca Nurse and Mary Esty.

Too many, too many! They smile and nod at me, and I act in kind. But they are like the ghosts of our crippled past. I ponder if this is such a good idea after all, seeing each other in this meetinghouse again.

We all must stand now. Ann Putnam walks up the aisle and turns to face us. Here is Reverend Green in the pulpit.

How old Ann has become! Why, she can't be more than onescore and six! And she looks so tired and sickly. I recollect now what they say of her, how her parents both died within a fortnight of each other several years past. And she has brought up her younger siblings.

She *is* done up nicely, in the whitest of caps and shawls. But I do not trust her motives. I never will. They say she would seek communion in this church again. I'll wager that's the only reason for her being here. Now she speaks.

Her voice is weak. I can barely hear her.

"I can truly and uprightly say, before God and man, that I did it not out of anger, malice, or ill will to any person, for I had no such thing against one of them; but what I did was ignorantly done, being deluded by Satan."

Her voice rings out, gaining in strength.

"I desire to lie in the dust and earnestly beg forgiveness of God, and from all those unto whom I have given just cause of sorrow and offense."

She goes on, but I do not hear her. My mind closes against the hearing.

What of Tituba, I think, who languished in prison long after others were pardoned because she could not pay her room and board? Only to be given, again as a slave, to a man who paid her fees.

What of Abigail Hobbs, once free of spirit and brave of heart, who confessed to witchcraft so as not to be left out and who, like many of the girls in the circle, now leads the life of a disreputable woman?

What of John Dorich, who one day simply boarded a ship at the wharf in Salem and disappeared? And what of little Dorcas Good, who went to prison at five and still roams our town homeless, her mind gone, muttering to herself and dressed in tatters?

I can never forget any of them, those poor souls who were hanged or whose lives were broken by the madness.

Reverend Green speaks now. His voice is strong and clear, and the words he uses are plain.

"None of us is wholly innocent in this tragedy. We seem to have forgotten what our fathers came into this wilderness to seek. The sealing ordinances of the covenant of grace and church communion have been much slighted and neglected by all that has happened. And all that lies upon our community still. Yea, the fury of the storm raised by Satan during that tragic year hath fallen very heavily upon many that lived here. Some say the Lord sent evil angels to awaken and punish our negligence."

Everyone's eyes are upon him.

"Let us now diminish the power of those evil

angels. Let us send them back, for all time, from whence they came. Will ye not do this with me here today? Will ye not soften your hearts now to this young woman who has thrown herself upon your mercy? Will ye not heal the wounds of this community for all time, for yourselves and for your children, by forgiving her sin?"

He comes down from the pulpit. "Stand now in your pews as she passes and reach out to her in forgiveness."

And so Ann approaches each pew. The people stand and reach their hands out to her, of course. But I sense they do it for Reverend Green—who has taken off his doublet and helped many to build new barns or till their fields—and not for Ann Putnam.

She comes toward me now. I stand. Would that I were not alone in the pew with the children. Everyone's eyes are upon me.

The look on her face is so stricken. She has dark circles under her eyes. It is as if death itself has a grip on her. I feel so strong, so robust, next to her. I feel my babe in my arms. I am mindful of baby Johnathan's sturdy little body beside me. And I know that Ann has no husband or child. God has been good to me, after all. With my free hand I reach out to her. She takes it in her own fragile one. Her hand is so cold!

"Susanna English," she whispers as if to an old friend, "how good of you to come this day."

She is surprised that I am here. And why would I not be?

"What lovely children. You are blessed. How is your Johnathan?"

"He is well."

"You forgive me, then? I am near death's door. The Devil has already picked my bones. I'll never have husband and children to hold close to me."

I feel something give inside me, like a great wall collapsing. And it comes to me that the hate I bore her all these years was more fearful than the person I was supposed to be hating. I can barely say the words. My heart is so full. "Yes, Ann, I forgive you."

We leave the church now. I walk with the children out into the golden August twilight. Curiously, I am light of heart. It is as if a protective mantle has been thrown about me, and yet, at the same time, as if the weight of an old wet cloak has been removed from my shoulders. I feel a sense of well-being I have not felt in years.

Johnathan and Elizabeth and Joseph, William and Juliette await us. Mary, who is fourteen now, is begging her father to allow her to go to sea the next time Johnathan and I take a coastal journey to Virginia or Maine with William. Elizabeth and Joseph have had four girls and one boy since 1692. They both want another boy.

"It is over." One of the kinsmen of Rebecca Nurse comes to shake Joseph by the hand and kiss Elizabeth. "We must allow it to be over. But we will never forget, Joseph, how hard you worked to stop the hangings."

"Others worked hard, too," Joseph says. And he looks at me. But to this day no one but Joseph, Elizabeth, and Johnathan knows of my part in the Brattle letter. I would keep it secret. And Joseph and the others honor my wishes.

We walk through the sweet August dusk to our carriages for the three-mile ride to Joseph and Elizabeth Putnam's for supper.

"Do you feel better for having gone?" Johnathan asks me as he helps me and the children into our carriage.

"Yes, Johnathan." I smile up at him. "You were right. It was good that we went."

We drive in silence for a while. But something in my heart needs saying. "Johnathan, I would speak of a matter we promised each other we would never speak of."

"What is that, Susanna?"

"Do you recollect that day we stood on the wharf in Salem Harbor when William came home?"

He scowls at me. Then he smiles. "You mean the name on the schooner?"

"Yes. Remember how we both stared, spellbound, at it?"

"The *Amiable Tiger*. Aye," Johnathan says. And he shakes his head and laughs. "Just as Sam Endicott said it would be. But we did promise we'd never speak of it, Susanna. Why give it mention now, after all these years?"

"You never told me what you thought of William coming home on the *Amiable Tiger*, Johnathan."

"No," he admits. "But I've pondered on it often."

"Can you tell me now what you think of it?"

"What think you, Susanna? That Mary Bradbury was a witch, after all? Or that Sam Endicott, being a seaman, knew what ship William was bound home on?"

I stare at him. Our eyes meet. And he smiles in that way he has, which still makes me weak in the bones. "I think that Sam Endicott knew because he was a seaman," I say.

"Are you sure, Susanna? Is your heart at rest, then?"

"No," I say. "I'm not sure. But I'll worry the matter no more, Johnathan. Nor should you. And we must never tell anyone that Sam Endicott knew what ship William would be on, lest this witch business start over again."

" 'Twill never start again," he says.

"Are you sure of *that*, Johnathan?"

He looks at me. "No, my love. For we've seen how easily neighbor can mistrust neighbor, and how a crowd can eagerly attend the hanging of one they've known all their lives. And how doubts can gnaw away at all solid thought, like a mouse at cheese."

I nod. "And how fear can take shape," I say, "and become more real than things one can see and touch. And plunge the heart down a dark road from whence one may never return."

He takes my hand. "We'll speak naught of the *Amiable Tiger*," he says. "Promise?"

I promise. For I know better than any that the line is thin between what is fanciful and what is real, and human nature being what it is, a witch hunt can easily start up again if we are not careful.

Author's Note

In the beginning of our country's history, young people shared in the daily chores and burdens of survival. Ofttimes they were not allowed a childhood. And many times they had a hand, in the background, in influencing history itself.

Research into the Puritan era shows that people went right from childhood into adulthood, with no benefit of an awkward age in between. An orphaned child was allowed to choose his or her own guardians at the age of fourteen; the laws applied to all persons of the age of sixteen, which was also the age at which boys were liable to serve in the military. On the other hand, the average age for marriage was twenty-two for women and twenty-seven for men.

Herein, as I see it, was laid the groundwork for the mischief that led to the Salem witch hunts of 1692.

History tells us the girls in the circle—from little Betty Parris, who was nine, to Sarah Churchill, twenty—were living in that social limbo that the Puritans assigned to their teenagers.

They had no amusements or entertainment. Music, dancing, and even the traditional holiday of Christmas were forbidden. Toys were nonexistent.

Anyone caught with a doll or "poppet" was suspected of practicing forbidden arts. Meeting on Sunday lasted several hours. Reading consisted of studying the Bible.

Moreover, winters were long and unrelenting. Is it any wonder, then, when the winds moaned around their houses in the winter of 1691–1692 and the dark came early and the wolves howled on the edge of town, that the girls of Salem formed their circle in the Reverend Parris's house, where his black slave Tituba lulled them with stories?

History tells us that to those stories Tituba added little sorceries, which probably included tea-leaf and palm reading—in other words, she indulged in the black arts.

There are many theories about the witch hysteria of 1692 and the trials that followed, not the least of which is that there was a virus in the rye that caused the afflicted girls to go into their fits.

That may account for their physical sufferings, but it has never been proven. And it only shows the extent to which Puritans were attuned to mystical powers: they considered these fits the work of the Devil himself.

The town fathers, magistrates, and ministers truly believed that the Devil was roaming the countryside looking for ways to undermine the kingdom of God on earth. The elders in Salem needed a scapegoat for their troubles in 1692. There had recently been an outbreak of smallpox, Indian raids on the fringes of town, and much bad feeling between neighbors who would not lay old quarrels to rest. And they all felt insecure because Massachusetts Bay Colony had lost its charter, which had assured them of their land grants.

So, then, there was the town, brooding under this social environment of suspicion and fear that hearkened back to the old days and the Old World, where putting witches to death was a tradition. All the ingredients for chaos were present.

When I decided to do this novel, I needed a protagonist, and I did not want one of the girls from the circle—for who could sympathize with one of them? I went to the Essex Institute in Salem, where I found the story of Philip English (I spell his name *Phillip*) as written by one of his descendants.

He had two teenage daughters. What intrigued me about the English family is that they were "outsiders" at the start, simply by virtue of being considered gentry. But more than that, Phillip English was enlightened enough to see the failures of Puritan society and to want his children to think for themselves.

It would follow, then, that Susanna English would not have been welcomed into any gathering of girls from the village.

I was further induced to make Susanna my protagonist because her brother, William, was lost at sea, and because history tells us that in later years she married the son of Magistrate John Hathorne. Hathorne prosecuted her parents, yet she married his son.

Why? No one knows why. I invented my own reason: because young Johnathan disagreed with his father over the witch trials and took the side of Susanna, for one.

But history also tells us that the descendants of Susanna and Johnathan Hathorne added a *w* to their name, making it *Hawthorne*. And that their foremost descendant was Nathaniel Hawthorne, who roamed the streets of Salem in his time, haunted by the part his ancestor had played in the witch trials. As a result, Nathaniel Hawthorne wrote *The House of the Seven Gables*, one of the classics of American literature.

I took liberties in my plot by having brother William return—when actually he was lost at sea— thereby building in a perfect reason why Susanna would want to meet Tituba, who told fortunes.

I wanted my protagonist to be someone who would know from the outset the cause of the witch hysteria, and Susanna English could do this for me. She would also not speak out for most of the story, having been threatened that her family would be named witches.

Almost everything about the English family in this

book, except Susanna's role in the witchcraft business, is true. Mary English did own a shop. The children did refer to Phillip as "honored Father English." Their father did row across the bay to St. Michael's in Marblehead because he was Church of England. His history, as a man of principle who stood for what he believed in, is authentic. Mary English did befriend Sarah Cloyce in church when Sarah was shunned.

Phillip and Mary English were arrested. They fled from Boston to New York with their daughters at the behest of Reverend Joshua Moody of Boston, who convinced Phillip English that justice did not await them in Salem. The undocumented story is that Sir William Phips himself gave them letters of introduction to Governor Benjamin Fletcher of New York.

It was my invention, for the sake of story, to have Susanna ask for and receive permission from her parents to stay in Salem. Sister Mary's marriage to fictional Thomas Hitchbourne, Susanna's stay with the Putnams, and Susanna's involvement in the letters of Reverend Pike and Thomas Brattle are all my own inventions. Pike and Brattle did write letters that led to the end of the witchcraft business, but historically they did so on their own. But if someone like Susanna stepped forward with information to encourage the letter writers, it could have been kept secret. No one really knows what individual small acts of courage contributed to the resolution of the witch hysteria in Salem.

We do know that Phillip English did send corn and flour to Salem from New York during the terrible winter of 1692–1693. And he did steal the body of Sheriff George Corwin after that man died.

I chose Joseph and Elizabeth Putnam as the family Susanna would stay with because history tells us that Joseph Putnam had the spirit of American independence even in that dark and unenlightened time. Historically, he did go to his brother's house and tell his sister-in-law, Ann Putnam, that if she touched anyone in his house with her foul lies, she would be sorry. And he did keep his horses saddled in the barn at all times, ready to flee with his family if arrested. From the outset, he did not believe in the witch hysteria.

In 1718, another son was born to Joseph and Elizabeth Putnam. Young Israel became one of the foremost generals in the American Revolution. Known as "Old Put," he was a member of the Sons of Liberty, and when news of the Battle of Lexington reached him as he was plowing his fields in Connecticut, he left the plow, unhitched a horse, and rode one hundred miles in eighteen hours to Cambridge, Massachusetts. He was in the battle of Bunker Hill.

History tells us that in 1692 there was a young girl named Abigail Hobbs in Salem who defied restrictions and lived in the woods and eventually confessed to witchcraft. And that John Dorich was one young boy the girls allowed to participate in their circle. That elderly Mary Bradbury was accused of haunting ships at sea but escaped is also historically accurate, as is my account of John Alden, who was accused of witchcraft, made a prisoner in his own home, and who eventually escaped.

I have used these characters at will, working with the facts documented about them and filling in my own motivation. The idea of making Joseph Putnam the leader of a Salem resistance movement against the witch hysteria is my own. There definitely was a core of people working to bring sanity back to Salem, and given Joseph Putnam's bravery and streak of independence, I decided to make him the catalyst in this movement.

In doing research, one discovers many things. I became fascinated by some of the similarities between the era of the Salem witch trials and today's world. Then, as now, if a person was well placed, like Phillip English, he could work out an arrangement to be allowed certain freedoms while under arrest. And those named as witches were often persons of "no account," like Tituba, who was a black slave; Sarah Good, whose husband was landless; Bridget Bishop, who went against the strictures of society; and others who were considered outcasts.

But most of all, I was intrigued by the idea that

you could "cop a plea" in those days, just like today. Those who admitted to the charge of witchcraft were allowed to go free, part of that deal being that they named others. Those who denied the charge were imprisoned.

Other intriguing facts my research uncovered revises the long-held opinion we all have about Puritans. They were not people who walked around in somber-colored clothing, denying themselves life's pleasures. Yes, they worked hard and spent long hours at Meeting. But they were human, they liked their fun, and they took it wherever and whenever they could.

One has only to delve into the court cases of the time or read current scholarship to learn that the power exerted over them by parents and ministers and magistrates was often in theory only. Episodes of behavior that went against community regulations are rife in court cases, which show constant trials and convictions for sexual offenses committed by both married and single persons.

Paternity cases, fornication, or in the instance of married couples, adultery, were all part of the social fabric of the times and common causes for concern. But even the known list of court cases does not take into account occurrences in which the parties did not get caught. And frequently the only proof was a child born out of wedlock, or a baby that was not full term, born to a couple after marriage.

In other words, the Puritans were people just like us. Except that their laws were stricter, and they had to be more inventive about not getting caught. Thus, I allowed Johnathan and Susanna to hold hands, to kiss, to be off alone on walks, under the distant approval of a benevolent Joseph Putnam.

As for clothing, here again we have harbored stereotypical views. Yes, jewelry was forbidden, as were some of the more outlandish headdresses, lace ruffs, and billowing skirts worn at the same time in England. But the fabrics used by the Puritans were varied. For warmth, many layers of clothing were necessary, and while black connoted authority and dignity, many colors were allowed in daily garb, from orange-brown to blue and green and yellow and purple. The tones were muted, however, since color was achieved from the use of vegetable dyes.

Why then, did Bishop's "red bodice," documented in history, get her into trouble? I put it down to the general atmosphere of intolerance that prevailed in Salem at the time—intolerance for everything and everyone who did not subscribe to the very repressive "norm."

I have formed my own theories about the witch trials. I believe the girls in the circle were caught in the web of their own mischief; that, having indulged in forbidden pleasures, they had to go along with the diagnosis that the evil hand was on them or admit to their activities, which would have incurred terrible punishment.

It makes sense to me that once the ministers and magistrates paid mind to every word the girls uttered, these teenagers could not let go of their newfound fame. Performing in Ingersoll's Ordinary, being excused from chores and from attendance at Meeting, being relieved of all the restrictions of a harsh society, they found power and notoriety they could not give up. So the witchcraft hysteria gained in momentum.

People were arrested, imprisoned, hanged. Then it was too late for the girls to speak out. Their jump to celebrity status could be likened to that of an ordinary teenager in today's world suddenly being on "The Oprah Winfrey Show."

And the whole business was fed by ancient beliefs and fears and local hatreds. Did not Ann Putnam, the younger, confess in 1706 that she had indeed dissembled?

One important aspect of the Salem witch trials of 1692 is that the people of Massachusetts Bay Colony—with the exception of Governor William Phips, who wrote two letters to England—solved the matter themselves.

And, although twenty-four people died as a result

of this hysteria (nineteen were hanged, one was pressed to death, and four died in prison), the elders of the colony eventually came to their senses without intervention from the Mother Country.

Using such facts, I wrote my story, but it is just a story. For the real facts about Salem during the witch trials, there are many scholarly books you can read. And you can visit the town of Salem, where you can explore the wonderful historic sites and form your own opinion about the witch trials.

Bibliography

A historical novel like this one would be impossible to write if one could not refer to the scholarly writings of men and women who have researched the period. The books and papers I used as references for this work are listed below. There are many more books to be read on witchcraft in England and America and on the time period involved in my novel, as well as original papers to be studied, if one is so inclined.

Original Papers

English, Mrs. Philip. 1943. "Facts about the Life of Philip English of Salem." Essex Institute, Salem, Massachusetts. Photocopy.

Books

Brown, David C. *A Guide to the Salem Witchcraft Hysteria of 1692.* Worcester, MA: Mercantile Printing Company, 1984.

Demos, John. *A Little Commonwealth: Family Life in Plymouth Colony.* New York: Oxford University Press, 1970.

Karlsen, Carol F. *The Devil in the Shape of a Woman: Witchcraft in Colonial New England.* New York: W. W. Norton & Co., 1987.

Leach, Douglas Edward. *Flintlock and Tomahawk: New England in King Philip's War.* New York: W. W. Norton & Co., 1966.

Morgan, Edmund S. *The Puritan Dilemma: The Story of John Winthrop.* Boston: Little, Brown & Co., 1958.

Richardson, Katherine W. *The Salem Witchcraft Trials.* Salem, MA: Essex Institute, 1983.

Rutman, Darrett B. *The Morning of America, 1603–1789.* Boston: Houghton Mifflin Co., 1971.

Rutman, Darrett B. *Winthrop's Boston: A Portrait of a Puritan Town, 1630–1649.* Chapel Hill: University of North Carolina Press, 1965.

Snow, Edward Rowe. *Disaster at Sea.* Three volumes in one: *Marine Mysteries and Dramatic Disasters of New England* (1976); *Sea Disasters and Inland Catastrophes* (1980); *Pirates, Shipwrecks and Historic Chronicles* (1981). New York: Avenel Books, Compilation, 1990.

Starkey, Marion L. *The Devil in Massachusetts: A Modern Enquiry into the Salem Witch Trials.* New York: Alfred A. Knopf, Inc., 1949; New York: Anchor Books, 1969.

Reader Chat Page

1. Why does Susanna feel she is as guilty as Ann Putnam and her circle of girls? Do you think she shares their guilt?

2. Father English advises Susanna: "Think for yourself, daughter. But know when to speak and when to remain silent." Susanna had many chances to tell what she knew about Ann's circle. Why didn't she break charity with the girls? Would you have spoken up in her situation?

3. Why did the magistrates believe the girl accusers?

4. Susanna claims that "ideas were never encouraged in Salem." Why might ideas be discouraged?

5. John Indian says, "If we waited all our lives to do what was allowed, we would never do anything." Is it ever a good idea to do things that aren't allowed?

6. Why would Ann and her friends fake possession by the devil and accuse innocent people of witchcraft? How do you feel about their reasons? Do kids today do cruel things for sport and attention? Who could you turn to if you knew about kids creating trouble?

7. Why did Tituba and other prisoners confess to a crime they didn't commit?

8. Susanna believes the townspeople will forgive Ann when she asks for forgiveness. Why would they? Would you?

About the Author

Ann Rinaldi is an award-winning author best known for bringing history vividly to life. Among her books for Harcourt are *The Coffin Quilt: The Feud between the Hatfields and the McCoys*, an ABA's Pick of the Lists, and *The Staircase*, a New York Public Library Book for the Teen Age.

A self-made writer, Ms. Rinaldi never attended college but learned her craft through reading and writing. As a columnist for twenty-one years at *The Trentonian* in New Jersey, she learned the art of finding a good story, capturing it in words, and meeting a deadline.

Ms. Rinaldi attributes her interest in history to her son, who enlisted her to take part in historical reenactments up and down the East Coast, where she cooked the food, made the clothing, and learned about the dances, songs, and lifestyles that prevailed in eighteenth-century America.

Ann Rinaldi has two grown children and lives with her husband in central New Jersey.